# CALL FROM THE DEAD

The phone booth where Joel Tinker and his life parted company stood alone at the empty end of a row of brick buildings.

"Right out in the middle of nowhere," Waku observed, scanning the area. "Must have used a high-powered rifle with a scope. Bet your friend never saw it coming."

"Oh he saw it coming," I replied heavily. "That's why he was in the phone booth in the first place."

We stared at the hills, bare white and devoid of any foliage. "Looks like the moon," Waku said. "What the hell was he doing in this town?"

"Running scared."

*Don't Miss the Other*
*Nestor Dark Mystery*
*by* **Arthur Rosenfeld**
*from Avon Books*

DARK MONEY

# DARK TRACKS

## ARTHUR ROSENFELD

AVON BOOKS ◆ NEW YORK

DARK TRACKS is an original publication of Avon Books. This work
has never before appeared in book form. This work is a novel. Any
similarity to actual persons or events is purely coincidental.

AVON BOOKS
A division of
The Hearst Corporation
1350 Avenue of the Americas
New York, New York 10019

Copyright © 1992 by Arthur Rosenfeld
Published by arrangement with the author
Library of Congress Catalog Card Number: 92-93070
ISBN: 0-380-76487-3

First Avon Books Printing: October 1992

AVON TRADEMARK REG. U.S. PAT. OFF. AND IN OTHER COUNTRIES, MARCA
REGISTRADA, HECHO EN U.S.A.

Printed in the U.S.A.

RA   10  9  8  7  6  5  4  3  2  1

# Chapter 1

THIRTY-CALIBER SNOWFLAKES WERE hitting the gray New York City sidewalks. The phone lines were alight with people needing Dark Foundation money to help them through the worst recession in a decade. Monday morning office work made me yearn for the days when I was alive and alert on the street with SWAT, worrying about nothing except whether I had my kevlar vest on and it would save me from the next whacko with a gun. And if wearing my cap backwards made me look as silly as the guys on television.

The intercom buzzed insistently. I didn't want to answer it, so I left my desk, went to the bookcase and pressed hard on the clothbound version of Dostoevski's *Crime and Punishment*. The secret door whirred and clicked, turning my bookcase into a portal to Dark Disneyland.

The toy room was bathed in a full-spectrum fluorescent glow. A stainless steel Walther PPK hung in midair in front of me, seemingly by magic, no strings attached. A "Z gauge" miniature electric train, the transformer wired into the light switch, gathered speed past shelves of remote control planes, cars, and boats, electronic gadgets, and rack after rack of fine air weapons. Just below and to the left of the levitating pistol, a shooting bench, muzzle clamps, and sandbags marked the beginning of an indoor firing range extending exactly ten meters to a set of targets on the far wall. Except for the hum of the trains and the whirr of electrostatic air cleaners the room was as silent as a tomb.

I selected a Feinwerkbau rifle from the gun rack, pulled back the side-cocking lever, and inserted a match-grade lead pellet. Smoothly and easily, I hefted the twelve-pound piece to my shoulder. I studiously ignored the flashing red light on the far wall that told me I was needed in the office, centered the distant black circle above the open sights, and executed the perfect squeeze that had once made me the sharpest triggerman New York's Finest had to offer.

Most people think that cops get off on a sense of control over others. I think it's the sense of order that seduces. My childhood had been chaos, but NYPD changed all that. Then Uncle Andrew died and left me hundreds of millions, and things went crazy again: everybody wanting something and I was conscience-bound to provide. I took pleasure out of ignoring the flashing red light, not because I liked to keep people waiting, but because I liked to have some control of myself.

Someone thumped heavily against the bookcase. I put the rifle down and reluctantly released the latch, allowing Charlie Bender, my best friend and the chairman of Columbia University's Artificial Intelligence Lab, to push his wheelchair into my inner sanctum. He gestured at the levitating Walther.

"Neodymium-iron-boron magnets?"

"Can't a guy have some peace and quiet around here?" I complained.

"I could have let myself in, you know. Pushed on *Crime and Punishment,* or some such thing."

I blanched.

"Ah, that's the one then, is it? Fitting for the guy who lives the dark life of a tragic hero. Things are tough, I know. Beautiful woman, all the money in the world, envy of all your friends."

"Leave me alone."

"Isabelle's got some environmentalist group waiting outside. You going to sulk like a spoiled kid, or you going to talk to them?"

I squeezed off another shot. It hit dead center.

"I see you're still sharp," he commented."

"I can't seem to get into the day. I'm missing the thrill of the chase."

Bender studied me for a moment.

"I thought you got that out of your system when you got that counterfeiter."

"That was months ago."

"You're bored."

"Boredom is an insult to oneself. I'm just restless."

Bender smiled, dug in his pocket and stretched out his hand.

"Here. Have a look at this."

It was a tiny camera, old-fashioned and finely wrought out of matchsticks.

"Very nice."

"You think there's a market for more?"

"Only if the population of dwarf photographers is growing."

Bender gave me a wounded look, and I followed him out to face the world.

\* \* \*

Before Isabelle Redfield answered my newspaper ad for a secretary—and ended up running both my heart and the Dark Foundation—she had made a living modeling her beautiful hands in nail polish advertisements. She spread those hands now, to great dramatic effect.

"I can't keep up with the phones, and the Gaia Leaguers have had all the carrot juice they care to drink."

"You give your guests *carrot* juice?" Bender marveled.

"Send them in," I sighed.

There were three of them, all wearing earth tones and looking like hippies. Isabelle introduced them as Peter Rogoff, Karla Kemp, and Sid Quarter.

"We use the term 'Gaia' to denote the concept of the earth as a living organism," Rogoff began.

"You have the lean look of the vegetarian," Quarter told me.

"Anyone who read the *Playboy* interview knows that. Forget sucking up to me. If you deserve Dark money, you'll get it."

"The article said you were a straight shooter," murmured Karla Kemp, a woman with big round glasses and wiry hair.

"You have no idea," Bender said under his breath.

"What keeps you from flesh?" asked Rogoff.

"I feel better when I don't eat meat."

"It takes a lot from the earth to make a cow," said Kemp. "We can't afford to waste the energy any more."

"I don't mean to be rude, but may we get to the

heart of your pitch? You can see by the telephones that Ms. Redfield and I are swamped.''

"The Gaia League believes that the earth is neither man's playground nor his garbage dump, but rather a gigantic, magnificent, and incredibly complex organism. Plants, trees, cockroaches, and people, as well as gold and platinum, caves, and icicles, are all parts of the whole,'' said Quarter.

"Like the various parts of the body,'' said Isabelle.

"Just so. The key principle of our theory is balance. When one element grows out of bounds, equilibrium is lost and the organism—in this case the planet Earth—must fight back. We believe she is doing that, with war, heart disease, famine, AIDS, deviant behavior, and other weapons at her disposal,'' said Kemp.

"Human population is out of control,'' said Rogoff.

"Like a cancer,'' added Quarter.

"All the environmental crises that we face, from radioactive dumping to polluted food, rivers, and seas, can be traced back to the fact that there are just too many of us,'' Rogoff finished.

I stared at them. "What do you propose? Genocide? Mass suicides? Worldwide sterilization?''

"We're not lunatics, Mr. Dark. We need publishing money to get the word out—with educational materials, documentaries, fliers, books. We need people to wake up and take notice before it's too late. Population control is only one part of the picture. Greater sensitivity to Mother Earth is equally critical.''

At that moment, I noticed a light on the far end of my phone, signifying that the answering service was trying to get through on the line I reserve for emergencies.

"Excuse me a moment," I said, and picked it up.

"You've got an emergency call from Tasmania," said the operator.

"Tasmania?"

"Australia, sir. A Dr. Joel Tinker. He says it's extremely urgent."

Everyone in the room looked at me expectantly. I held up my hand.

"Put him through."

The voice came faintly across many thousands of miles.

"Nestor?"

"Joel? What the hell are you doing in Tasmania? I thought you were working for the Bronx Zoo."

"How could you forget? I'm here on your money!" his voice sounded thin, faraway, and desperate.

"Ah yes, hunting for an extinct tiger or something—right?"

"That's what everyone thinks, but *they're* wrong. Look, Nestor, I've got to be quick about this; I don't have much time. Somebody's trying to kill me."

"Why would anyone want to kill you?"

"I don't know!" his voice went up an octave.

"Have you been to the police?"

"Of course. They think I'm nuts, told me to bring them proof. I don't even know what that means. Nestor, I didn't know whom else to call."

"Where are you right now?"

"A little town called Zeehan. At a pay phone. Look, everything I've discovered is in my notes. I've express mailed them to you for safekeeping."

"Why don't you get the hell out of there? Hop the first flight home and we'll talk about this."

"I can't just . . . you don't understand. It's wild here; I'm nowhere near an airport; I'd have to drive;

they're too close. It's the Tasmanian tiger, Nestor. It's *not* extinct. They know I've found it, and they're after me.''

''Nobody's after you. Look, give me the pay phone number.''

Suddenly the static on the line was gone.

''Joel?''

Mile after mile of undersea cable hummed faintly in my ear, but the tiger hunter was mute.

# Chapter 2

I TOLD THE Gaia League that I had to deal with an emergency, and I rescheduled their appointment. I needed time to think about their ideas before I could grant or deny them Dark money. I asked Isabelle to have my chauffeur, Waku, fire up my stretch Benz.

"Your friend is dreaming," Charlie Bender announced when we were alone. "The Tasmanian tiger has been extinct for decades."

"Not if Joel Tinker says he's found it."

"Who is this guy, anyway?" asked Bender.

"High school best buddy. Science whiz like you, but into strange animals. Brilliant, and very precise. I've got to get up to the Bronx Zoo and check this out. Give you a lift?"

"I'll stay here and flirt with Isabelle." He winked.

The door to my private elevator opened into the building's underground garage. Waku was wearing an impish smile.

"You in a hurry?" he asked hopefully.

"Yes. Bronx Zoo."

Waku is an Australian aboriginal whose idea of the big time was pimping in Brooklyn, until I turned him into an informant. He left the street just after I did, when my uncle's money changed my life. He loves to drive fast, figuring that because I was once a policeman he can't possibly get a ticket. He gets proved wrong now and then, but it doesn't make any difference.

"What do you know about Tasmania?" I asked him as we swung onto the East River Drive.

"It's an island off the southeast coast. Foreigners don't go there much. It's beautiful—mountains, beautiful beaches. Forty thousand years ago there was a bridge linking it to the Australian mainland."

"How about more recent history?"

He looked at me in the rearview mirror.

"Lots of white men killed lots of black men in Tasmania. The whites linked hands and walked across the island, driving my people into the sea. Some were just political prisoners or victims of the class struggle, but most were criminals. The worst of England's worst."

"And the Tasmanian tiger?"

"In the days of my grandfather they were everywhere. Now they're gone."

"Extinct?"

"Must be, Detective. No more left."

Traffic across the Willis Avenue Bridge and onto Bruckner Boulevard was light, and before we knew it we were up the Bronx River Parkway and taking the Boston Road exit to the zoo.

Joel Tinker's boss was Stanley Winston, the zoo's director of research. Although we had never met, he knew all about the Dark Foundation grant, and of my friendship with Joel.

"We don't let too many people drive their stretch limos down the zoo path." Winston smiled, coming around his desk to shake hands.

"You should have made me get out and walk," I replied, smiling back. "All I get to do these days is sit behind a desk."

"It's not every day that a man like you comes to the zoo, Mr. Dark, and quite frankly, as Joel Tinker's boss, I owe you one. That research money from your Foundation may make us all famous some day soon."

"Speaking of Joel, when did he last touch base?"

"He calls in every week and reports at least as often by mail. He called last Wednesday, but I wasn't in, so I guess we spoke the week before that. His reports are very encouraging. I think he may actually be on to something."

"He called me today," I said, glancing at my watch. "About an hour ago."

"He called *you?*"

"He's in trouble, Dr. Winston. In fact, he sounded terrified. Afraid someone is trying to kill him."

He listened carefully while I related the call in detail.

"This is totally out of left field," he said, puzzled.

"Frankly, I'm worried. Joel's not the hysterical type."

"I'd have to agree. He's emotional, gets excited enough about things for me to have to rein him in sometimes, but I don't see him as paranoid."

"Could you tell me a little bit about his project?" I asked.

"I've always viewed it as a romantic fantasy, far too speculative a venture for our budget. Without your money, he wouldn't be over there now. But his reports have surprised me. If the Tasmanian tiger really *does* exist it will be front page news.''

''How is this tiger different from the Asian species?''

''It's not a tiger at all, really. Some people even call it the Tasmanian 'wolf.' Better to call it the thylacine, from the Latin name. It is, or was, a marsupial, the largest carnivorous marsupial to live into modern times. About the size of a large dog, with jaws and habits similar to a hyena's. Like all indigenous Australian mammals—the dingo dog, the rabbit, and the fox were brought to the Red Continent—the thylacine carries its young in a belly pouch.''

''Sounds like a four-legged, meat-eating kangaroo.''

''If that helps you picture it, yes. Thylacines preyed heavily on sheep, and wool farming is critical to the Australian economy. Bounties were set, and the thylacine was blasted into oblivion by rifles. A tragedy, really. Good fencing would have done it. As far as we know, the last one was seen in the wild in 1908. A captive male lived in captivity at the Taronga Park Zoo in Sydney until 1933. It really is considered an extinct species. That's why Joel's work is so exciting.''

''What made Joel think to look?''

Winston sighed. ''Tasmania is a unique environment. Mountains, plains, and very thick temperate rain forest. Beautiful hardwoods grow there, although they're being decimated by the day, and men spend lots of time in the bush. There are sightings now and then, and there are still hundreds of thousands of inaccessible acres, particularly in the rural southwest of the state. Some people believe the tiger is hiding there, in national parkland, far away from anyone and anybody.''

"Like finding a wooly mammoth in suspended animation, or maybe the Loch Ness monster,'' I said.

Winston gave me another one of his rueful smiles.

"You sound just like Joel Tinker.''

I had an appointment with an engineer who had developed a new style of roller blade based on a high-tech teflon bearing. The young woman wanted Dark money to develop the skate, but I was more interested in the industrial potential of the bearing. We were on the highway headed back to the Foundation office when the phone rang. It was Isabelle, and she sounded worried.

"I have Captain Rignola on the line,'' she said. "It sounds urgent.''

Years ago, Giuseppe Rignola was my commanding officer in Special Weapons and Tactics. He was envious when my financier uncle, Andrew Dark, died and left me his fortune, furious when I quit the force, and apoplectic when I took Waku off the street to be my right hand man. The other guys were glad for me, though, and during the last several years, Rignola and I had developed a good working relationship. He found that when it came to picking certain fruits, my arm had grown longer than his, and I found a powerful police contact invaluable. He wouldn't be calling unless it were important.

"Patch him through,'' I instructed.

Rignola's voice came over the line a moment later. There was no video image. NYPD doesn't budget for toys.

"You know a guy called Joel Tinker?'' he asked.

"I know him,'' I said, suddenly cold.

"Well they just found him in a telephone booth in some place called Tasmania. Had your card in his wallet. Local PD traced the last call made from the booth and it rang your office in New York. Interpol contacted me."

"What happened?"

Rignola took a deep breath. "Front of his head had a nice little hole in the cheek. You don't want to know about the back. Guy's deader than hell, Nestor."

# Chapter 3

AN EXPRESS MAIL package came from Joel the next day. A brief cover note said he was sending it to me for safe-keeping. It contained field notes and biological details of his work. His death moved me hard as I looked them over. He was a close friend, and an old one, the sort who drifts in and out of your life but is always there, in the background. Friends like Joel are forever, and, as the saying goes, they ain't makin' any more.

"You're just doing this to get away from me," Isabelle teased.

"Don't be ridiculous. He's doing it because he's bored. For God's sake, Nestor, you don't need to go to Tasmania! What good will it do your friend now?" Bender quipped.

"No grant from me, no trip to Tasmania. No trip to Tasmania, no bullet in the head," I answered.

"Typical Dark-think. He does a guy a favor, and then he feels guilty about it," said Isabelle.

"I'm not feeling guilty about the favor. I'm feeling

guilty about the fact that the guy is dead! He was really something. You would have liked him.''

''At least not anymore,'' said Bender.

''You're both wrong,'' Waku chimed in. ''The detective is going to Australia because he wants to catch a tiger.''

It took Waku an hour and ten minutes to drive me to Ivor Sikorsky Memorial Field at Bridgeport, the airfield closest to my Redding, Connecticut home. Waku did his customary walking inspection tour of my Beechcraft Starship while I did my preflight check on the high performance craft. His tour was thorough. Aboriginals are highly spiritual people with a deep distrust of technology. They believe they can fly without airplanes. They believe the rest of us should be very careful.

As satisfied as he was going to get, Waku reappeared and topped off my supplies while I filed my flight plan to Santa Barbara. Most Starships are custom-built, and mine is fitted out like a Winnebago rather than a conference room. Autopilot notwithstanding, it's hard to hold a meeting when you're flying the plane, and I like to put down at unexpected fields at unorthodox times. The Starship's my ultimate escape.

Isabelle had arranged for me to pick up the night Qantas flight out of LAX. I could have taken American Airlines from JFK in New York and waited at Los Angeles, but I decided to fly myself out. It would be tight, but I could stop at my house in Santa Barbara to pack some things and still make it.

The Starship features a canard wing and twin pusher props, and provides a safe, fast, high-performance ride on less fuel than a Lear or a Gulfstream. I used to say that its design appealed to my minimalist nature, but I don't claim that any more because Isabelle ridicules me. She hates the plane, partly because once I nearly died crashing it, but more because it generally takes me away from her and indulges my self-absorbed and irresponsible streak.

I departed Connecticut and headed west over New York State, Pennsylvania, Ohio and then out across the Midwest. With the plane on autopilot, all that was required of me was a periodic look at the gauges and regular contact with air controllers when I overflew their traffic areas. I touched down at my favorite refueling field at Lincoln, Nebraska, then rose again full of avgas, Bach's Brandenburg Concerti blaring over the Starship's lavish stereo system. The brilliant, intricate melodies serenaded the rise of the Rockies out of the black-and-white patchwork of the plains states, then the southern deserts, and finally the broad blue beacon of the Pacific.

My ties to Santa Barbara, like my ties to so much else in my life, come courtesy of Andrew Dark. My uncle had exquisite taste and the resources to indulge it. Isabelle calls the West Coast home "The Hospital" because it's so spartan, but I understand that Uncle Andrew wanted it spare so he could think undistracted. I always look forward to spending time there.

When I finally arrived at land's end, the tower welcomed me home, and the Starship created the usual sensation on the field as I taxied to my tie-down. I ordered a fuel service on the radio, closed up the plane, and headed for the taxi stand. Before I could get out of the terminal, an effete-looking man in a gray business suit approached me.

"Mr. Dark?"

"Yes?"

"I'm Fleming. With Exotic Auto Specialties? I have a wonderful surprise for you, sir."

I was tired from the flight, but not too tired for this.

"The deal went through?"

"Just this afternoon, sir."

"Does that mean the Virage is outside?"

Fleming allowed himself a smile.

"I contacted your office and spoke with your assistant, sir. She told me that you just happened to be *en route,* so I took the liberty. . . ."

I pushed past him out the door at a jog. It's not every day I get a new Aston Martin. In fact, this was only the second car I'd bought since inheriting my uncle's money. The first was a Ford.

The Virage stood gleaming at the curb, its slender black flanks exuding poise, power, and exclusivity. When I was done admiring it from a distance, I stepped up and ran my fingers lightly over the thick black lacquer. Fleming handed me the keys.

"All yours, sir. Drive it in good health, and do bring it round for a service before a thousand miles. Get that break-in oil out of the pan."

"Who bought my Corniche?" I asked as I unlocked the driver's door and stared at the classic black-and-white gauges and the exquisite burl.

"A lady, sir." He coughed, embarrassed.

"Anybody interesting?"

"I shouldn't think so, sir. It was her ninetieth birthday present to herself."

"Will she take care of it, do you think?"

"Her dog died, sir. She had him stuffed and put him in the back window."

I started to smile, but then I thought of Joel Tinker, and the world turned gray, grim, and busy.

# Chapter 4

I DROPPED FLEMING off at the dealership, then drove to the stark whiteness of "The Hospital" for a hot soak before the trans-Pacific flight to Australia. I threw some outdoor clothing in a duffel, tossed the bag in the trunk of the Virage and headed down the Ventura Freeway. Ordinarily I would fly the hundred miles to Los Angeles International Airport in a matter of twenty minutes, but the allure of the new Aston Martin was too strong to ignore.

At Oxnard I freed myself of the late afternoon traffic and detoured west for the Pacific Coast highway. There was no time to break the car in among Malibu's endless winding canyons, so I stayed by the ocean, the Virage right at home among some of the world's most expensive real estate.

I passed helmetless teenagers in leather jackets on 170 mph motorcycles and an almost endless array of surfboard-toting pickups and minibuses, the transportation of choice for slaves of the perfect curl. The Virage raised a few eyebrows from Porsche drivers,

**and** garnered me several fresh applications of lipstick from drivers of Jaguar coupes that chased me from stoplight to stoplight.

When I had heard enough of the throaty growl of the fuel-injected 400 horsepower V-8, I set the compact disc player on replay and heard Joe Cotton's "Here I Am, Baby" over and over until the seaside two-lane ran out and I headed inland for LAX.

I left the Virage in the care of a specialty parking service near the airport. They locked it and covered it, protected it with plastic bumpers, and gave me the keys. I slept in the Qantas VIP lounge until the flight was called, took my duffel aboard, and stretched out in the first class section atop the Boeing 747 SP for the fourteen-hour stint to the arid crown of the Southern Hemisphere.

A dark-haired flight attendant with full lips, perfect teeth, and minty breath awoke me in the middle of the night to serve me dinner. I told her I was sure she had a vegetarian meal for me.

"Your name?"

"Nestor Dark."

She scanned down a list created on an old style dot-matrix printer, then shook her head.

"I'm sorry, sir, I don't see your name."

I shrugged and tried to go back to sleep, but she kept staring at me.

"Excuse me, sir? You wouldn't be, um, *the* Nestor Dark? The philanthropist who flies his own Beech-craft?" she said at last.

I sat up, stunned, and looked at her. For a moment I wasn't sure which surprised me more, being recognized as a philanthropist, or being recognized at all. Even after six years with Dark money, thinking of myself as anything other than an NYPD sniper took conscious effort.

"I read about you in a flying magazine," she confessed, bending closer in the aisle. "I'm studying to be a private pilot myself. In fact, I'm going for my instrument rating this month."

"You found me out," I said.

"Why don't I see if I can scavenge some broccoli and carrots from the other trays and make you a vegetable plate?" She squeezed my shoulder and was gone.

Although he had raised me as his own after my parents died, Andrew Dark rarely took me traveling, and never took me overseas. My journeys took place later, especially in the first year after his death from cancer. Then, rich and newly free of SWAT and nursing duties, I roamed the world to better prepare myself to follow my uncle's bidding and "do something good" with his money.

Among the skills I developed in my round-the-world spree was a surefire method for beating jet lag. I ate lightly, drank huge quantities of water, abstained from alcohol, took high doses of B vitamins, and used warm-up routines gleaned from years of kung fu to stay alert and limber.

The first class lounge was too small and crowded to allow me to move freely, so while my meal was being prepared I went downstairs, through business and coach classes, to the open space behind the crew seats near the lavatories in the tail section. There I began to systematically stretch my body, beginning by standing on one leg, cupping the other ankle in my hands, and rotating my foot. Next I stretched my calves in a deep, squatting runner's stretch, then my groin in a Chinese split, and finally my hips and hamstrings with deep, rotating twists. I had just begun to loosen my waist when the door from the toilet behind me opened and Waku emerged. Our eyes met. He looked sheepish.

"What the hell are your doing on this airplane?" I demanded.

"Isabelle sent me along. She thought you might need help in Australia. You know how she gets when you're not around."

When we arrived in Sydney I slung my carry-on bag over my shoulder and went straight past the conveyor belt. Waku held up his hand for me to wait.

"You checked baggage?" I asked.

"Some equipment for you."

I didn't like the look on his face.

"What kind of equipment?"

"Not so much. Two trunks."

"Two trunks!"

Suddenly two airport cops appeared carrying a pair of green trunks I recognized all too well. I looked at Waku in horror.

"How could you put my weapons chests on an international flight?" I hissed as the burly cops drew near.

"Captain Rignola helped with a special man at Kennedy Airport. I put the bags in your name."

The cops arrived and made it clear they knew who we were. We followed them into a private search room. I handed over my passport and immigration card while the cops hefted the trunks up onto the table. I unlocked the first one.

"Understand you were a SWAT man once upon a time," the first cop said as he stared at the sniper's rifle and the assortment of scopes, butt plates, and tools that accompanied it.

"Once upon a time."

He lifted the rifle tray out of the trunk and set it on the table. A 9mm Smith and Wesson "Performance Series" semiautomatic and an Uzi machine pistol and various holsters and grips came into view.

The second man whistled.

"Just here to put another shrimp on the barbie," I smiled.

"You going to catch them with a nine-millimeter pistol?"

I shrugged.

"What's in the other case?"

"I can only guess. My driver packed it for me."

Waku gave his best version of a disarming smile. The cop ignored him and opened the second case. The top tray was filled with ammunition. The first cop opened a box and withdrew a rifle cartridge that looked like a needle.

"Just what the hell is this?"

"Seventeen Remington. Flies straight and true and fast. Four thousand feet per second. Hell on shrimp," I said.

The man reddened and removed the tray to expose a dazzling spread of electronic surveillance and communications equipment. He picked up a unit that looked like a walkie-talkie.

"Two-way radio?" he inquired.

"You must be very highly trained," said Waku.

The cop drew a deep breath, restored both trays, closed the trunks.

"You here to start a war, Mr. Dark?"

"Maybe he packed me a little heavy."

"Then as a courtesy to Interpol we'll let you go

about your business and store these at no charge.''
He looked me in the eye and held open the door. It
was not time to push my luck, so I went through it,
fantasizing all the while of ways to dismember Waku.

When we got outside, I drew a deep breath, but
Waku stopped me before I could say a word.

"You worry too much, Detective. Makes your heart
weak. Kill you young."

He clicked his overnight case open just wide
enough for me to see a Walther P-88 auto pistol
equipped with a laser sight, a custom-built "take-
down" .223 Anschutz sniper rifle.

I didn't know whether to laugh or cry.

"How did you get this through security?"

"I told you the captain had a special friend."

"I know, but *carry on?*"

"You *still* worrying?"

Winter in New York meant summer in Sydney, and
by the time we reached Waku's brother's home in the
Ultimo district even the breeze off the famous harbor
and the shade of the ubiquitous gum trees couldn't
stop the raging sun.

"My brother is a fighter for aboriginal land rights.
An activist. He will find us help in Tasmania."

The cab pulled up in front of what appeared to be
a warehouse, and we got out. Waku slammed his hand
three times against the corrugated tin door, and it
swung inward on creaky hinges to reveal his precise
antipode. Where Waku was lean, his brother was fat;
where Waku was hyperalert, his brother was slow and
deliberate. Waku's hair was cropped close; his brother's hung down to his shoulders in a dusty black veil.

"I'm Nestor Dark." I offered my hand when they
were finished embracing.

He took it enthusiastically.

"I'm John. I've heard about you for years, Mr. Dark. I want to thank you for everything you've done for Waku."

"He's done plenty for me."

John's home belied its exterior. There was a fine courtyard behind the neat living room, replete with flower pots and a table, white plastic chairs, and a red umbrella advertising Foster's Lager. John gave me a background in Tasmanian politics while Waku played with a four-year-old nephew he had never met.

"Tassie's a strange place," John related, raising his glass in my direction. "It started out as Van Diemen's Land, a living hell for prisoners and the few of my people that were left alive. So many ghastly things happened there—I mean truly terrible, horrible things, Mr. Dark—that some people believe the entire island is haunted."

"Haunted!"

"At the prison at Port Arthur they carried out dissections on blokes that were still alive. White men beat each other senseless, starved each other, prayed for death. The native Tasmanians didn't look like me and Waku. They had smaller heads and different hair. The last one died in 1876. Most of Australia is warm in winter, but not Tasmania. Aboriginal people there used to walk through the snowy mountains wearing only grease. Where are you going first?

"Hobart," I answered.

"Pretty town. It looks a little like Sydney, red roof tiles and all that, but it's cold and socially dull. Sydney's an ethnic melting pot, but everybody in Hobart looks, thinks, and eats the same."

"And the tiger?"

"There is no tiger. You are here to avenge the death of a friend, am I right?"

"I'm not sure there's any avenging to do."

"I will ask someone special to come find you and help. Her name is Julie. Tasmania is beautiful, Mr. Dark, just don't ask the wrong questions."

I left his home ready for a clean bed and a sleep that would turn day into night and back into day again.

# Chapter 5

ONE OF AUSTRALIA'S seven states, the island of Tasmania sits in the middle of the "Roaring Forties," Southern Hemisphere latitudes infamous for fierce winds and the harsh, unpredictable weather they bring. The island is separated from the mainland by a hundred-mile stretch of ocean known as the Bass Strait. It's rough water, making for a nauseating overnight ferry trip from Melbourne. Many travelers opt either for the faster "jet cat" or a quick flight into one of Tasmania's three major airfields.

In the morning, Waku and I arranged to travel separately and rendezvous in Hobart. Exhausted from his nightlong reunion with his family, Waku was only too glad to circumvent airport metal detectors and relax in a comfortable chair aboard the fast boat.

I made the quick commuter hop from Sydney to Melbourne and then watched the gray of Australia's most industrialized metropolis dwindle beneath the eighteen-passenger DeHavilland Dash-8 turboprop and give way to the whitecaps of the Strait and then to the most spectacular coastline, beaches, and farmland I had ever seen.

I rented a car and drove into town. John's description was accurate. Hobart's capacious harbor and red tile roofs lent it a superficial resemblance to Sydney, but it lacked the bigger town's cosmopolitan feel. The people *did* appear to be of homogeneous British stock, but John hadn't mentioned that they would seem so relaxed and healthy. There was obviously something right about the Tasmanian lifestyle.

Following a map, I made my way to the central police station, where Waku had said a Lieutenant Pennington was expecting me. The lieutenant was slight, mustached, and sandy-haired. He showed me into the glassed-in cubicle that served as his office and offered me a seat. He was very curious about Joel Tinker's notes.

"We found an express mail receipt addressed to you on the body. I'd like to photocopy whatever he sent you while we chat," he said.

"It was a personal letter, and I don't have it with me. How is the investigation progressing?"

"Interpol has stepped up the pressure on us since you became involved, but I'm afraid we haven't made much progress. We do get tiger hunters here from time to time, although mostly it's the locals who show the treasure hunter mentality. We don't think much of it. There hasn't been a verified report of a thylacine since 1922. The last-known tiger died in captivity in 1936. A lot of fuss over nothing, if you ask me."

"Joel Tinker was an American scientist and a good friend of mine. He was killed in your state, and I want to know why. Do you have any idea who would have benefitted by his death?"

"The existence or extinction of the thylacine is an

environmental issue, Mr. Dark, and as such is politically charged. I'm sure you've heard about our trouble with the 'Greens.' ''

"I know that you have an active environmental movement."

"They're subversives, Mr. Dark. They're seeking political and personal power through the dismantling of Tasmania's economy. Our natural resources are all we have. Mineral mining, particularly copper, is our largest source of income, followed by timber and hydroelectric power."

"From dams?"

"We have some of the most advanced technology in the world."

"What about tourism?"

"A distant third. I'm all for keeping a place for a man to go fishing or take a walk in the woods, but the Greens would like to turn the whole bleeding state into a park. They don't even want airplanes to fly over the bush for fear of scaring birds or ruining a hiker's 'wilderness experience.' ''

"Where does the thylacine fit into all this?"

"It's a rallying point. Since nobody can prove that they *don't* exist, the Greens can always claim that any move to dam a river, pollute a stream, or clear a forest would take the species over the edge. Now, about that letter?"

"It was strictly personal and irrelevant to the investigation," I replied.

"I would certainly appreciate a peek, mate," Pennington said, adding his best broad smile.

"Joel's work was done under the aegis of the New York Zoological Society. He made reports to that organization. Dr. Stanley Winston at the Bronx Zoo should be able to furnish them."

"He already has," Pennington answered. "The last entry is three weeks old."

I spread my hands.

"I understand you're a very wealthy and well-connected man, Mr. Dark, but you're in Tassie now, and you're a hell of a long way from home. Things go easily for you in your protected little world, with your money and your connections and all. It's different in Tasmania. People like people with the right attitude here. Even the weather can be dangerous."

"That sounds a hell of a lot like a threat."

"I'm just suggesting that we cooperate with each other, that's all."

I shook my head, stood up and collected my things.

"It's a question of principle then, is it, Mr. Dark?"

"You know what, Lieutenant? The longer I live, the more I find that almost *everything* is a question of principle."

I was afraid that Waku was late because he had been apprehended with our weapons, but the booking agent assured me that he would be in by late afternoon, just as soon as some minor engine trouble was taken care of. I spent the time doing a little research at Hobart's prime tourist attraction, the collection of shops at Salamanca Place.

"Tasmanian blackwood," an overfed furniture salesman said proudly, indicating a dark and richly-patterned coffee able. "It's our finest."

I pointed to a light-colored credenza.

"Huon pine," he said. "Also unique to the state. Very famous for building ships. Convict laborers used it last century. It won't rot, you see. The oil inside kills fungus and bacteria. We've got lots of other pines that don't grow anywhere else: the King William, celery top, pencil, cheshunt, creeping, oyster bay, south esk, and looseleaf.''

"Only pines?''

"Lord, no! I already showed you the blackwood. Eucalypts dominate the rain forest, but we've got sassafras, myrtle, native plum.''

I found a small, uniquely-sculpted sassafras footstool and bought it, then moved on to a second-hand bookshop. I prowled around the shelves and stacks for at least half an hour until the proprietor—operating on Tasmania time—finally put down his newspaper and shuffled my way with the gait of a bookworm.

"Have anything on the thylacine?'' I asked.

"This and that.''

I ended up with an excellent monograph, as well as a series of hand-drawn color plates, fine works of the last century, done on tightly-woven paper and showing a strange-looking reddish brown beast with black stripes. It looked more like an animal out of an illustrator's imagination than so recently real and extinct a creature. The hindquarters were distinctly kangaroo-like, as if they had been grafted on to the forepart of a big dog by black magic. The mouth was slightly agape in the drawing, the teeth dripping saliva, the eyes bright with killing purpose. I tried to project myself into a past where it had roamed free and easy, but could only think about Joel Tinker.

# Chapter 6

IT WAS 3:00 P.M. when Waku finally arrived, and we headed north and west towards Zeehan, the town where Joel Tinker died and the most logical place to begin retracing his footsteps. Our route took us out of Hobart along the Derwent River valley. The rental car agency had given me an Australian-built Ford Fairlane, a V-8-powered car similar in dimension to my Taurus SHO and with almost as much torque. Medium-sized by American standards, the car dominated the slender Tasmanian blacktop, making left-hand driving even more difficult. I went wide on one turn, just past the town of Ouse, and nearly slammed into a log truck coming the other way.

"Goddam road's flat as a go-kart track," I cursed. "No banking."

"Time for me to drive, Detective," Waku said.

I promised to give him the wheel at nightfall, and pursued the narrow road through spectacular expanses of farmland that reminded me of Switzerland. The horizon offered up the distance in tantalizing detail, and each breath of air through the car window was mango sweet. Waku explained that the Southern Hemisphere gales kept Tasmanian air ultra-fresh.

"Cape Grim, on the northwest tip, has the cleanest air in the world," he said.

"How come you know so much about Tasmania?"

"I did a little reading on the plane," he confessed.

The occasional burst of dense eucalypt forest revealed that the farmlands had once been temperate rain forest glades. As we neared the center of the island, the flatlands gave way to rolling hills with thick patches of pines erupting like garden shoots. More serious mountains followed, and the road twisted and turned through these, the patchwork of black earth and snow making a magnificent mosaic. At Tarraleah I veered off the main road and prowled the streets looking for something to eat.

"Regular ghost town," said Waku.

Waku was right. There wasn't a soul on the streets and the houses appeared empty; interiors visible from the car revealed nary a painting nor a stick of furniture. A ten-foot green pipe ran along the roadbed.

"Water. There must be a pumping station nearby," he said.

We tried Tarraleah's only inn, but were told by a surly hostess that supper time had passed. From what I'd seen, I was surprised she wasn't doing cartwheels to get the business.

"If we can't have dinner we'll take tea," I told her, choosing a corner table.

The waitress—when she finally arrived—had a much sunnier disposition.

"It *is* after nine, but I've some vegetable barley soup left if you want it."

We ordered a couple of bowls and had half finished

them when two lumberjack types walked into the dining room and started inaudible small talk with the hostess. They nodded often in our direction until the bigger one finally wandered over. I wasn't happy about it. I'd seen his look before.

"Help you with something?" I asked.

"What's a Yank doing in Tarraleah?"

"Just passing through."

"Hope you're doing the driving, Yank. *He's* likely to put his toes on the wheel."

"Actually he's quite a good driver."

"Can I see your tail? I hear your mother fucks kangaroos." Waku smiled sweetly.

Waku's a pretty good street fighter. He's had to be to survive as a hundred-and-forty-pound pimp. But it would take more than savvy to make up the seventy pounds between him and the big lumberjack. He tried elbows and knees like I'd taught him, but sagged quickly into the timberman's bear hug, a writhing ball of angry flesh getting the life and air squeezed out of him in an eyeball-popping hurry.

The other man made the mistake of joining in the fun. He wound up his fist to take a shot at Waku's chin right about the time I landed a carefully measured blow to the side of the neck. The hostess wailed and Waku's captor winced. Waku would have grinned if he could breathe.

"Let him go," I said.

The big man leered and squeezed harder, so I kicked his cheek with my shin bone, missing Waku by millimeters.

"Good thing I got a fast head, huh, Detective?" Waku grinned, shrugging the man's limp form from his shoulders like an oversized winter coat.

"Your head's fine, it's your mouth that's a problem."

\* \* \*

We headed out of Tarraleah on the main road, Waku
at the wheel.

"Bad road," he commented, looking for headlights in the mirror, avoiding my eyes.

A few minutes later we began a steep, hairpin de-
scent toward a glowing sky. I checked the map.

"There's not supposed to be another town until
Brady's Lake," I said, puzzled.

As we grew nearer, the glow resolved into the lights
of a massive hydroelectric station, the brightly colored generators and yellow-clad maintenance men
clearly visible through a wall of windows.

At that moment a set of headlights appeared on our
right, and a pickup truck came thundering towards us
from a dirt feeder road. A shotgun barrel appeared
from the side window.

"Duck!" I screamed.

By the time I was two years out of SWAT, things
between me and Captain Rignola had cooled to the
point where I was able to persuade him—at the cost
of whispering to the mayor my opinion about a certain
police equipment budget—to let Waku take the NYPD
evasive driving course. Whether this helped, or
whether Waku would have instinctively known that
buckshot can't follow a serpentine path frankly didn't
matter. All I cared about was that he suddenly pitched
the Fairlane into a series of careening maneuvers,
driving first hard left, then hard right, two wheels
often on the shoulder as the shotgun thundered inef-
fectually behind us.

"Where's the Walther?" I gasped.

"Trunk," he answered, concentrating completely
on the road.

We were directly opposite the power station when

a Toyota loaded with men suddenly appeared from the power station lot and made to cut us off.

"Maybe I shouldn't have reminded that man about his mother," Waku said, spinning the wheel and crashing the woven wire gate into the power compound.

The big V-8 howled as we made for the back of the station at full throttle, coming to a stop behind a row of steel trash dumpsters. We opened our doors simultaneously and Waku sprinted for the truck, key outstretched, just as the pickup truck roared into view. I heard a sound like heavy hail as buckshot hit the trunk lid. Waku tossed me the weapons case and ran behind the dumpsters. We heard brakes, then voices. I tossed him back the P-88 and a box of ammo.

Waku filled the clip and rammed it home. I screwed the barrel on the Anschutz, loaded, and emptied two boxes of shells into my pockets.

"We can't stay here," I panted.

Car and truck doors slammed, and a heavily accented voice called out to us to come out quietly with our hands up. I pointed to the space underneath one of the dumpsters. Waku nodded. I reached over the lip, gently raised the lid and felt around until my fingers closed over an empty beer bottle. I pulled it out as quietly as I could, then tossed the bottle overhead in the direction of our assailants.

A centerfire bullet vaporized the glass in midair as Waku and I rolled underneath the dumpsters, came out the far side, and made for the plant, crab-walking to stay in the shadows.

The shooters wised up when we didn't appear and split into two groups, one pursuing us, the other heading us off by going around the building. I knew it would take time for them to circle completely around, so I motioned Waku to press himself against the wall, put my eye to the night scope, and assumed a sniper's kneel.

I took the first two out with head shots just as the third located the muzzle flash. He managed to spray the concrete near my knee with one short burst from his autopistol before my .223mm caught him right above the heart. The bright red fountain told me in an instant that I'd ruptured his aorta. He died with his hands clasped to his chest trying to staunch the flow in a gesture as futile as a prayer. Waku ran up to him, took a good look and hurried back, the Walther in his hand.

"Orientals," he hissed.

# Chapter 7

WE RAN AROUND to the rear door of the plant and slipped inside. The noise was deafening. Keeping as low as possible, I ran from generator to generator, the smooth wood of the Anschutz stock in one hand, the warm barrel in the other. Waku stayed within my shadow. Several times we slipped around a control aisle just in time to avoid discovery by one of the yellow-suited technicians.

The final dash to the front door threatened to blow our cover.

"We have got to do it," Waku whispered. "There's no other way out."

I nodded, watching the men at the control panel make notes on clipboards and turn an occasional dial. When all backs were to us, we sprinted, but somebody saw us and began yelling. We were out the door before it mattered, running flat out along the edge of the building.

Waku ran for the Ford as soon as he saw the dumpsters, and I had to launch a flying tackle to bring

him down. He struggled under me, angry and confused. I let him up, put my finger to my lips.

"It's a setup," I hissed. "They wouldn't leave their
cars alone."

We crept closer and I knelt and crisscrossed the
target area with the nightscope. A short, stocky man
with an Uzi smoked a cigarette near the Ford's empty
trunk. The orange glow from his hand lit his almond
eyes like twin chandeliers. I trained the .223 on his
throat.

"Too much noise; you'll give us away," Waku
whispered.

I lowered the rifle and we split up. I went wide to
come around by the pickup, while Waku went straight
in under the protection of the dumpsters. When I saw
that he was in position, I took a gamble. I raised my
hands and stood up so that the cigarette smoker could
see me.

"Don't shoot! I have Tinker's letter," I called.

His one moment of confusion was enough for Waku
to bring the butt of the Walther down on the thug's
skull, and he crumpled. The instant he was on the
ground, Waku sliced the two truck tires with his knife,
then did the same thing to the Toyota. I recovered the
travel bag from where I had shoved it, briefly checked
that its contents were intact, and slid into the front
seat of the Fairlane. Waku clicked the trunk closed
and got behind the wheel.

"No keys!" he whispered, fumbling at the steering
column.

I'd barely gotten my fingers into the vest pocket of
the man I had just taken out when I heard the Fairlane's V-8 roar to life. I dove through the door as
Waku turned the car around. We sped away into the
night, following the white line by the light of the

moon. We drove the shot-up Fairlane as far as Derwent Bridge before I told Waku to pull the car off the road and into the shelter of some scrub. I got out, kicked over the tire tracks with my feet, and we reclined the seats and slept in the car, awakened twice by police sirens and once by the crazy cackle of a kookaburra out on the town.

The next morning, Waku drove west in silence while I fiddled vainly with the AM dial for news of the previous night's shootout. The only proof that anything had happened at all were the streaks of lead inside the barrel of the Anschutz and a couple of creases along the Fairlane's trunk.

"You feel bad," he said.

"I killed three men yesterday."

"They were going to kill you."

"I feel bad, not guilty."

"Who were they?"

"Japanese. I understood a word or two."

"You've helped them on their journey."

"I'm not sure I believe that."

"You've got a choice of what to believe. Why believe what makes you feel bad when you can't prove things either way?"

We sat quietly for a time. I searched for evidence in the fabric of life around me that would help me believe that goats and bugs and men came back over and over again in different bodies, or that the men who had died with lead in their heads and hearts were off on a journey and I had given them a leg-up.

"Why would Japanese be after the notes?" Waku asked, breaking the long quiet.

"I don't know."

"Do they contain a secret?"

"Maybe."

"The tiger?"

"If there is one."

"You going to call the police?"

"The police already know."

"Why do you say that?"

I took a long, deep breath. "You think the boys at the inn have Japanese friends with automatic weapons?"

The road led west through increasingly dark, damp and foreboding terrain, bisecting Cradle Mountain Lake St. Clair and Franklin and Lower Gordon Wild Rivers National Parks. After a time the lush landscape turned more and more barren, until Waku stopped the car so we could get out and take in the view.

"Looks like a nuclear testing area," I said, staring at the hills, bare white and devoid of any foliage.

"Looks like the moon," said Waku.

Descending into the valley, we passed an industrial complex I recognized as a mine, then came into a small town. Waku pulled in to fill up. A lanky teenager was working on a dolly underneath a milk truck. He rolled out to pump the gas.

I asked him about the scenery.

"Didn't you read your travel book, mate? This is Queenstown. Place looks like the moon because all the hills are dead from the sulphur. They've cleaned the place up a lot now, but it used to be a bloke couldn't breathe for more than about twenty years before his lungs shriveled up and killed him."

"Why don't they plant some trees?"

The boy shrugged. "Town council likes it this way, says it makes us unique. *Most* tourists know all about it, drive all the way out just to have a look."

"We're tiger hunters," said Waku.

"Haven't been any tigers since my grandpa's day," said the boy.

We got back in and drove on to the mining museum and handful of stores that passed for a town called Zeehan.

"Major metropolis," I said.

Waku pointed out an old cemetery built down a dirt road off the main highway, the decrepit tombstones rising woefully against a backdrop of blue mountains.

"They put your friend in there?" he asked.

"No. They shipped him home."

"That means you're going to miss the funeral, doesn't it?"

"I've never been big on funerals."

The phone booth where Joel Tinker and his life had parted company stood alone at the empty end of a row of brick buildings. I got out, stretched, walked over. Waku joined me, knelt, and ran his finger over a dark stain in the concrete. I stared numbly at Joel Tinker's blood and thought about his face in high school, his first attempt to grow a beard, about the girls he liked, about his wild science projects.

"Right out in the middle of nowhere," Waku observed, scanning the area. "Must have used a high-powered rifle with a scope. Bet your friend never saw it coming."

"Oh, he saw it coming. That's why he was in the phone booth in the first place," I replied heavily.

"What the hell was he doing in this town?" Waku wondered aloud.

"Running scared."

The only community of any size on the entire west coast of Tasmania, Strahan would be a bland and unimpressive little town were it not for its spectacular setting on Macquarie Harbour, one of the largest and most agreeable in the southern hemisphere. Violent and changeable weather, and a nearby dramatic, wave-battered ocean beach distinguish it still further. It takes a pioneer spirit to choose Strahan as a home, and that's exactly what we found in Graham Pullman, proprietor of Macquarie House, the bed and breakfast establishment Joel Tinker had used as his Tasmanian base of operations. Pullman had an athletic frame, open expression, and startlingly clear blue eyes that seemed to demand honesty and candor by merely settling themselves on my person.

"Quite a lot of fanfare preceded you, Mr. Dark. I've heard from your assistant, Dr. Winston at the New York Zoological Gardens, and, of course, the Tasmanian police."

"I hope I won't disappoint," I said.

"I'm very sorry about your friend, Mr. Dark."

"Thank you. So am I."

Pullman looked me up and down with a blend of concern and mild amusement. I decided that I liked him.

"I hope you don't think me rude, but you look as if you've slept in your clothes. Did you have a rough drive?" he asked.

"You should see the car," Waku interjected.

I introduced them, and we carried our bags inside. From the exquisite stained and beveled glass on the front door to the hardwood banister on the winding staircase, Macquarie House had been restored in high Victorian style.

"This is one beautiful place," said Waku.

"You really have done a beautiful job," I concurred, looking approvingly about.

"It took years of work, lots of money—which I hope to make back when you tell all your American friends the treasure we have here in Strahan—and the efforts of my chef and generally indispensable Czech helper, Divac."

As if on command, a strikingly handsome man appeared in the door wearing chef's whites and an apron.

"Divac, I'd like you to meet Mr. Dark and his driver, Mr. Waku."

Waku and I extended our hands, and Divac looked at them warily.

"You will forgive me, I hope, if I do not shake hands, but I am cooking your lunch. You are hungry for lunch, yes?"

Divac's expression told me he wasn't going to be overjoyed I was a vegetarian.

"Better not be meat," said Waku. "The detective doesn't eat meat."

"It is fish," Divac replied icily, fixing Waku with a stare.

Pullman intervened. "We have a number of fine fish in Tasmanian waters, Mr. Dark. Most are antarctic deep ocean varieties harvested by our local fleet. Divac has prepared you what he considers the best of them, orange roughy. I find it quite tasteless, but Divac's sauce is, of course, exquisite."

"It is only tasteless to a tasteless man," Divac replied.

"We could have had the salmon," Pullman teased with a smile.

"Mr. Dark doesn't eat fish," said Waku.

"I didn't know there were salmon in Tasmania," I said, trying to change the subject.

"Best in the world, according to the Japanese. They pay twice the price they'll pay for any other salmon.

They say our fish tastes better because the water's unpolluted.''

''The Japanese again,'' muttered Waku.

''*You*, I assume, will eat fish, Mr. Waku?'' asked Divac pointedly.

''At least they haven't offered a reward for the salmon,'' Pullman said.

''What does that mean?'' I asked, looking hard at Pullman.

''The tiger money, of course,'' he answered. ''The Japanese have offered five million American dollars for a thylacine, dead or alive. I was sure you knew.''

# Chapter 8

"You won't find Tasmania an easy place to be a vegetarian," Pullman cautioned, over an excellent lunch of native plants served by a grumbling Divac.

"But there's farmland everywhere," I responded.

"Like most of the rest of Tasmania, our farmland is owned by giant corporations. Local produce is sprayed, frozen, and packaged for export before even the farmhands can eat it. What's on your plate comes from our own garden."

It was a delicious lunch, and I told him so, loudly, so that my remarks would carry to the kitchen. Waku paid little attention to the entire exchange, as he was busy devouring a beautiful fish filet.

"About the reward," I ventured when half of my vegetable plate was gone.

Pullman dabbed his mouth delicately with his napkin. "You are, of course, familiar with the Christian doctrine which suggests that man has dominion over Earth and all the creatures therein?"

"It's the predominating Western view. I'm familiar with it, but I don't necessarily agree."

"Neither do members of our Green movement. The Japanese, however, take the whole concept to new heights."

"Rhinoceros horn," Waku interjected, his mouth half full of fish.

Pullman smiled faintly. "Precisely, Mr. Waku. The Japanese have an ongoing appetite for delicacies provided by creatures of all kinds, and engage in the pursuit of exotica as a sort of one-upsmanship."

"You're saying Japanese like trophies," I ventured.

"The rarer the better," Pullman answered.

"And what could be rarer than a thylacine?" I pursued.

"Nothing. It's extinct."

I was standing at the window of my room at Macquarie House when Graham Pullman knocked on the door and came in bearing some of Joel Tinker's personal effects.

"I thought you might want these," he said, handing me a beat-up stainless steel Rolex Explorer Two wristwatch, a billfold with a few Australian dollars in it, and a small pile of clothes.

"Thanks."

He nodded and asked if I felt like talking. I didn't, but I said I did.

"I was told you were coming here to retrace Dr. Tinker's steps. Is that correct?"

"More or less."

"But you had no knowledge of the reward?"

"I'm not here to find the thylacine. I'm here to find out who killed my friend, and why."

Pullman joined me at the window, made a sweep of the distant harbor with his hand.

"Beautiful, isn't it?"

"It's full of contrasts, like everything else in Tasmania."

He gave me a genuinely puzzled look.

"The beaches, for instance. They're the most beautiful I've ever seen. Nobody's footprints but my own, mile after mile of perfect, tantalizing sand, but waves too big to swim in."

"Yes, I see what you mean," he smiled slightly. "Tassie's not perfect. That's part of her charm."

"And the roads," I said, feeling slightly mean and angry towards the strange land where an old friend had died and I had nearly joined him. "The scenery's beautiful, but the roads are idiotic. Built by farmers, probably, not engineers."

"They're awful," he concurred.

"At least you've got a wonderful harbor. Hundred and ten square miles. Second biggest in Australia, I'm told."

"Were you told that to get through it you've got to master crashing surf, deadly sandbars, and a tide that will pull you right out to sea with the motor running?"

"No."

"That wasn't the worst of it," he said. "The seaman's nightmare was just the beginning of the bad dream. See that little island out there?"

I looked, nodded.

"Sarah Island. And the rock next to it? Grummet Island. Those two little landings comprised the most brutal colony ever established by the British."

"I thought the nasty prison was built at Port Arthur on the other side of the island."

"That was bad. This was worse. Thirty-three thousand seven hundred and twenty-three lashes given to a hundred and sixty-seven prisoners in four years."

"I'm going to have to see it all. I want to go everywhere Joel Tinker went."

"He shared the details of his hunt?" Pullman looked surprised.

"He sent me some notes," I said carefully.

"No wonder the police couldn't find those. They searched his room quite thoroughly."

"He mailed them to me in New York. Look, I'll need a boat. I have to go out on the river. Can you arrange it?"

"I'll take you myself. In the morning."

That evening I called Isabelle at my home in Connecticut. The trans-Pacific telephone cable crossed the international date line, allowing me to speak to Isabelle from a day I hadn't seen yet.

"I'm glad to hear your voice. I miss you," she said over the background static.

"I miss you too. How's my dog?"

"He doesn't eat for me like he eats for you."

"Can you see ribs?"

"He hasn't lost any weight, Nestor, you've only been gone a couple of days. What have you found out about poor Joel? What does it look like there?"

"I'm cold all the time. I thought it would be warmer. Waku and I got shot at by some Japanese."

"What?"

"I need you to do some things for me. Will you get a pencil?"

"Miles ahead of you. Are you all right?"

"We are; they're not. Get ahold of Rignola. Tell

him that some Japanese conglomerate—or maybe an individual trophy collector—has a five million dollar reward out for the tiger. I'm sure Interpol's already working the angle, but I'd like to know who it is.''

''You think they'll try again?''

''Not right away. We gave them a run for their money.''

''Jesus, I hate that *macho* shit, Nestor. Why don't you just let the police handle it?''

''I think the police started it.''

''That makes me feel much better.''

''What's happening businesswise?''

''A Mr. Johannsen faxed a proposal for a new type of home air cleaner for allergic people. He's been calling every day for an appointment.''

''Tons of those around. What's different about his?''

''It's cheap. Replaceable filter. Runs on solar energy. Needs to be near a window. No electricity.''

''Solar energy. I like it. Call him back and set it up. What else?''

''Dr. Winston called from the Bronx Zoo, wanted an update on the investigation.''

''Tell him to call Rignola directly. Be nice about it. What else?''

''A weird one. I know, I know, you love the weird ones.''

''Well?''

''There's a guy with a gadget that he says heals the brain with tiny electric currents. Says it can also be used to produce a relaxed alpha state in the brain, eight to twelve hertz, whatever that means.''

''Just a measurement of current. Does he have studies?''

"Anecdotes, but I heard some of them, and they're pretty convincing."

"Of course they're convincing. He's a salesman. That one will have to wait."

"When will I see you?"

"How soon can you get here?"

She inhaled sharply. "You want me to come to Tasmania?"

"No, I want to stay here indefinitely, cold and lonely, while you live in my house, feed my dog, and run my foundation."

"You're such a shit, Nestor. I give you the perfect opening for a romantic comeback and you screw it up."

"If I was perfect, you wouldn't love me."

"If you were perfect, I wouldn't *recognize* you."

# Chapter 9

MACQUARIE HARBOR IS fed by by two major rivers. The King empties into the northern half of the inlet after following a course that takes it near the Queenstown moonscape. The wider and more significant Gordon, a riverine nirvana, originates with the Olga and the Franklin in the wild, uninhabited southwest and fills the southern basin. The King River, long the toilet for Queenstown mines and smelteries, gushes vile chemical runoff into the harbor.

It was the area south of the junction of the Franklin and Gordon rivers which figured so prominently in Joel Tinker's notes of thylacine sightings, and it was there that I proceeded the next morning by boat, with Waku at my side and Graham Pullman at the helm.

Graham's boat was elegant, a fishing trawler stripped of her nets, towers, and other business equipment and finished tastefully in brass and teak to match the look and feel of Macquarie House. She measured fifty feet from stem to stern and drew a deeper draft than I would have thought ideal for river cruising.

"The harbor would take a liner, and the river's deeper than you think," Pullman observed, puffing furiously on a briarwood pipe that reeked of peach tobacco. He squinted through the bridge glass and the fog and guided *Phantasm* away from her mooring beside the inn and out across the scudding whitecaps of the harbor.

"Did you name her?"

"She's my boat," Pullman replied, shrugging his sou'wester up over his shoulders.

"Why *Phantasm?*"

"My romantic side, I suppose."

It took us just about an hour to cross the bay and make our way to the mouth of the Gordon. When we entered the shelter of the delta, the landscape changed dramatically. Waku leaned over and put his finger in the water and tasted it.

"Tannic acid?" he asked.

Pullman nodded. "Some root plants that grow along the banks give it off. Colors the water, but you can still drink it. Cleaner than what you get in New York, I'd warrant."

We proceeded slowly up the Gordon. Looking into the depths I saw the clouded sky reflected as perfectly as by a clean mirror's rendering.

"The famed Huon pine," Pullman said, gesturing at the gnarled bough of a tree that ended in surprisingly dainty needles. "Worms and rot won't touch it. Finest shipbuilding wood in the world."

"So I've heard," I said.

Waku was on his knees staring deep into the water.

"Can't see the fish," he said, getting up at last.

"They're in there," said Pullman.

He cut the engine and we drifted in blissful silence.

I heard Waku inhale deeply, and unconsciously I followed suit. The air tasted sweet.

"Amazing to see such wildness in an industrialized Western nation," I observed.

"The whole southwest has been a hotly contested area. Some years ago there was a big fight over a proposed dam on the Franklin River. Hydroelectric power is important to the economy. Tasmanian power stations feature some of the most advanced technology in the world."

"We've seen one up close," I interrupted.

"The dams are big projects. They make lots of jobs. Most of the potential sites have been dammed by now, but not the Franklin, thank God. The Greens stopped that by blockading the machinery, even went to the water in rafts. Made a human chain. Very dramatic. It's a fragile ecosystem here."

"I understand that logging is a big issue, too," I said.

"It isn't so much the logging of specific large trees in moderation that people object to, it's the clearfilling. That's the utter devastation of an area for only a portion of the timber. Cheap, but lots of waste. They chip, too, to make pulp for paper. The pulp mills give off heavy metals and organic bleaches, deadly to the environment. We don't have mills in this area, but we've had to fight to keep the loggers out as well as the dammers. Riverbanks like we're seeing now are very delicate. Myrtle root systems hold the soil together. There's only ten inches of it. The boat's wake could ruin it; that's why we're going so slowly."

"And the thylacine?"

"The southwest is very inaccessible. Tigers really could be in there. Anything could. The timber makes it too thick to really survey properly. There are a few diehard trackers who've been all through it, but mostly it's free of man.''

''You wouldn't be one of those trackers, would you?'' I asked Pullman casually.

He just smiled, pointed to a gum tree among the pines.

''That's the myrtle. Probably two hundred years old.''

''If tigers are in there, what do they eat?''

''Probably pademelons. That's a kind of wallaby.''

''Small kangaroo,'' Waku explained.

''How exactly did Joel Tinker hunt the beast? Did you take him downstream on this boat?''

''Initially I did, just to give him the lay of the land. Later he went off on his own. Don't his notes describe that?''

''They talk about where he went, not how he got there.''

''I believe he went up the Gordon some. You know he went in by float plane?''

''Now, that sounds like an idea,'' said Waku.

I wandered aft from the bridge and watched the reflection of the perfect sky in the black water grow denser and more foreboding. The scattered clouds congealed on the tapestry before me, but the image was ruined by a thousand tiny little disturbances on the surface as the rainclouds arrived and let loose on me and the river and the boat and the trees.

Isabelle arrived at Strahan that night by way of Devonport on the north coast and a bewitched and overeager representative of the Tasmanian police. She came in a truck loaded with three large crates and some personal luggage I knew to be full of goods even the wily Waku could not have gotten through customs. I watched from my room at Macquarie House as the cop left her at the door, satisfied by a squeeze from her hand and a smile that took the chill off his night. An utterly charmed Graham Pullman greeted her at the door of the inn and directed her upstairs.

Her luggage preceded her through the door of my suite, as did the smells of her; intimate smells that followed after her as well, wisping and wafting about the door and her things and the meat of her. I took her in my arms.

"I have to shower, Nestor. That was one hell of a long trip. I'm probably growing mold."

She put her model hands on my shoulders, looked me full in the eyes and pushed me gently away, smiling.

"I want some," I said.

"You want some what?"

"Mold. Let me help you out of those filthy traveling clothes."

"I know your kind of help, and you'll just have to wait!" She laughed, backing towards the bathroom.

I followed, but she was saved by a knock on the door.

"Probably Santa Claus with your toys," she said, and slid off to the shower, closing the door behind her.

I admitted Waku and the bags.

"Pullman stored the crates behind the hotel," he said.

He started to unpack, pulling an 11mm Wildey—the finest, most powerful automatic pistol money could buy—out of a suitcase.

"Holy shit, I've never seen this one," he said.

I pried the massive pistol from his hand.

"You've got the Walther, so you've got nothing to bitch about. The Wildey's mine."

He stared, transfixed by the golf-ball-sized hole in the barrel. I checked to make sure the chamber was empty, then aimed the laser sight at the wall and squeezed the trigger gently. A tiny red beam appeared. Satisfied, I put the pistol away before Waku could get himself into any more trouble.

Next came a pair of Leitz field binoculars, known for their exceptional sharpness and light-gathering abilities. I used them to look out the window, and when I turned around, Waku was holding my NVEC 600 night vision pocketscope in his hand.

"What's this, a camera lens?"

"The latest nightscope. Lets you see in the dark, even without stars.

Waku unpacked the Buck V-52 selector knife, a system of seven blades and one handle.

"Nice," he said, running a thumb gently over the blade. He put down the knife and picked up the Kioga whip, a telescoping rod of spring steel that extended to two punishing feet with a mere flick of the wrist.

"Maim but not kill, right, Detective?" Waku asked, flicking it open and pushing it shut.

I snatched it away from him and went on to withdraw a four-foot custom-built remote control submarine.

"What the hell you going to do with that?"

I checked the fins and propellers and the little ballast engine, all controlled by the tips of my fingers on the intricate control panel. The blades made a humming noise when they spun, biting air instead of the black water that would soon surround them.

"Hunt," I answered.

Next I unpacked the video bag. There was a Sony Super-8 inside with a variety of lenses and stands.

"You going to take pictures of the woods?"

"You know damn well what I'm going to take pictures of," I answered. He just smiled and slipped out the door as the knob to the bathroom turned.

Wisps of wet blonde hair clung to Isabelle's face as she peeked to see if we were alone. Satisfied, she came out, rivulets of water sliding down her slender calves. She was wearing my bathrobe, the part above the drawstring hanging loose and open so that I could see her breasts.

"It's cold in Tasmania, Mister Dark. And I don't see an electric blanket."

"I was reading the other day how male odors control female hormones in mice," I said.

"You read too much," said Isabelle, gliding across the room, catching my hand and taking me to the bed. "And you talk too much, too."

The moon was bright and the trees cast variegated shadows across the clean white sheets, making dark creases in Isabelle's perfect white body, creating recesses where there were none, challenging me to distinguish the real from the imagined. I burrowed and nestled and kneaded and caressed, and then it was her turn and we tried hard to keep quiet lest people downstairs hear all the excitement and start rumors I'd never live down.

# Chapter 10

THE NEXT MORNING was thick with rain. Isabelle and I slept late and breakfasted alone at the big table. I had cracked wheat cereal and she ate a miniature egg soufflé prepared by Divac and served in a little earthenware cup. Divac, like Pullman, was enchanted by Isabelle.

"I thought you were just a boring vegetable person, Mr. Dark, but now I see you are a man of taste." He beamed at Isabelle.

She smiled back and complimented the soufflé.

"You understand that with the soufflé, as with love, timing is everything. If it is withdrawn from the oven a moment too late or a moment too soon, it falls limp and lifeless in the dish," he responded.

Isabelle ignored him. I attacked my cereal with vigor.

When we were finished eating, we watched the raindrops fall on Pullman's lush garden and listened to the trilling of Tasmanian tree frogs. Isabelle drank coffee while I prepared my own brand of stimulant, Siberian ginseng tea.

"You think Joel's death is tied in with the reward?" she asked.

"Joel's murder."

"All right, Joel's murder."

"Likelier that it is than it isn't."

"Rignola doesn't know a thing about it."

"That's bullshit, too! The reward's common knowledge. Why can't Interpol find it?"

"Maybe there *is* no reward."

At that moment a striking aboriginal woman with chiseled cheekbones and closely cropped hair appeared in the doorway. She was slender, willowy, and perfectly proportioned, with brilliant yellow eyes, long fingers, and equally long toes visible in sandals wet from the rain and streaked with short pieces of green grass. She was nearly as tall as Waku, who stood behind her.

"Oh, there's a reward all right. You'd find that out soon enough if you came up with a tiger," she said, stepping inside.

Isabelle fixed her with the knowing gaze that beautiful women reserve for each other.

"This is Julie Iringili, my brother John's friend. She's from Darwin. That's way up at the top of the mainland," said Waku.

I shook her hand and asked her what brought her to Strahan.

"My ancestors," she replied.

"She's been studying a cave way down the Franklin River. She's taking me to see it," Waku explained.

"How are you getting there?" I asked.

"I fly a Cessna floatplane," said Julie.

"Got room for two more?" I asked.

Julie looked down at our breakfast as if our diet would tell her what kind of people we were.

"The cave's a sacred site. Tasmania lags behind other Australian states in recognizing aboriginal land rights."

"You have every right to be bitter. But if you'd like to share it with us, we'd *love* to see the cave," said Isabelle.

Julie gave her just the barest hint of a smile and Waku slumped with relief.

We took off from the dock across the street from Macquarie House. Pullman and Divac watched as we loaded the remote control submarine into the aft cargo hold. I had to remove the conning tower, the nose section—where the ballast electronics were sealed in a compartment half the size of a shoe box and protected by silicon "O" rings—and the tail section that held the batteries.

"What's it supposed to do?" Julie asked, fascinated.

I promised her she'd find out.

The wind picked up as Isabelle and I climbed into the back seat and buckled up. Julie furnished us all with headsets and chin mikes, while Waku went out on the strut, turned the plane slightly, then scrambled aboard as the pontoons slapped the scudding harbor whitecaps. He closed the door behind him. Julie turned her attention to the throttle and trim.

We took off to the south, then banked eastward. I watched the detailed ripples and waves fade with altitude into an indistinct tableau as Julie called her flight plan into Melbourne.

"Why Melbourne?" Isabelle half-shouted into the mike over the throbbing din of the engine.

"Nearest major airport," Julie shouted back. "They'll have our flight on their logs. They don't hear from us after awhile, at least someone will know where we went."

She was an excellent pilot, and clearly understood how to handle the extra weight and peculiar aerodynamic characteristics of an aircraft with pontoons. She kept a light hand on the yoke, adjusted her mixture often and her trim wheel with precision, and seemed utterly oblivious to the fact that we were flying straight for a cloudbank.

"You instrument rated?" I asked after a time.

"We're not likely to run into anyone else flying low over the Franklin and Gordon Rivers in a cloud, but the answer is yes."

Suddenly the airplane lost five hundred feet in an instant.

"Mama," said Waku.

Julie smiled, regained control easily and handed back a stack of airsick bags. "Record for my passengers is six," she said.

We followed the course of the Gordon as it wound east and then made an abrupt turn south at the end of the Eagle Range. The entire network of creeks and mountains, rivers and gorges, stood out like a beautiful velvet relief map, the sun sending brilliant vertical shafts of light through tears in the fabric of the sky.

"We have the Greens to thank for the view," Julie observed. "If the hydroelectric company had its way, this would all be under water."

I related to Waku and Isabelle what Pullman had told me of the blockade. Julie nodded, pointed out the dam site. It was indeed inconceivable that anyone would deliberately ruin the magnificent wilderness below us.

"Is everything below us thylacine habitat?" I inquired.

She pointed down to a light green break in the underbrush.

"Thylacines are big animals. They used to go after sheep in clearings like that one. The sheep were easy prey there, but so were the tigers."

Instead of making straight for the cave, Julie flew along the watercourse to the junction of the two rivers.

"The Franklin River," she pointed out.

We banked gradually north to a place along the Gordon River where the granite banks rose steeply, black curtains obscuring the white water from every angle except directly overhead. The river widened some, and Julie throttled back.

"You're not going to land *here?*" Isabelle asked weakly.

Julie smiled distantly, intent upon the work her feet and fingers and arms were doing, charting and estimating and feeling and knowing all in her head. She changed her pitch so that the propeller bit less air, and the plane began to settle towards the water.

The sound from the Cessna's engine grew thinner and fainter as we dropped faster and faster. Then we were even with the tops of the intimidating black cliffs and then beneath them, into the gorge, the white water rushing beneath us so fast it seemed to be challenging us to a race, yipping at our pontoons like a neighborhood dog after the mailman's boots. I had confidence in Julie's flying, but there seemed no clear landing spot until we banked sharply to accommodate a bend in the river, then dropped onto a smooth black surface where the river widened and rested quietly from its tortuous course over the rocks. The pontoons hit with barely a splash, and Julie throttled back to idle, nosing the plane expertly to an area of soft soil where the myrtle roots had rotted away.

Isabelle clapped her hands in pleasure, and Waku opened his door and hopped out without prompting, jumping off the pontoon with the tie line in his hand. He waded to secure it on a tree stump while Julie cut the engine.

"A rainbow," Isabelle said softly.

The propeller feathered to a stop and we stepped out into a world that was blue and red and yellow all at once.

I could almost reach out and touch the pot of gold.

# Chapter 11

ISABELLE EXTENDED HER hands so far I thought her fingertips would come off. I took her in my arms, and she leaned back against them and closed her eyes. The filtered sunlight played across her face.

"Aboriginal legend holds much about rain, but very little about rainbows," said Julie, as she checked the knot that secured the Cessna to the bank.

She led us inland, away from the plane and the water, until the undergrowth obscured the sky. The dank, earthy smell of the temperate rain forest we had seen from above was like an enormous blanket, comforting in its closeness, but at the same time smothering. We walked a bit further, and it grew dramatically darker. I looked up and noticed that thirty feet above the ground the trees were interlinked by a carpet of horizontal branches. I pointed them out to Julie.

"Horizontal growth," she explained. "It's a species all its own. It grows at right angles to the trees and forms a tangled web that catches anything that falls from the treetops. It's like a second forest floor, thick enough for a man to walk on.''

We came upon the cave without warning. It hid behind a veil of ferns, looking like a huge fireplace. Julie stopped at the mouth, gray stalactites behind her.

"We're about to enter somebody's home," she said quietly, her yellow eyes burning like warning bulbs. "Please respect it. Maybe they'll return some day."

I took up the rear and we filed in, ducking between the rocks. The interior was surprisingly warm, and roomy enough to shelter a couple of dozen people from the unforgiving Tasmanian winter.

Waku bent and picked up a piece of flint that had been worked into a tool. He examined it a moment, then bent again and came up with a bone from the cave floor. It was as thick around as a human femur, but shorter, with different articulating surfaces.

"Tiger," he said simply.

Julie glanced at it, nodded. "It's a midden, a trash heap near a fire. This cave is the southernmost known habitation of human beings anywhere on earth in the last twenty-five thousand years. There were plenty of tigers then."

"It's like a tomb in here. Everything's so perfect," said Isabelle.

I tried to imagine the immense span of time that separated us from the day when little children had clung to their mother's legs, their small heads and tightly curled hair pressed against her strong black thighs, and feasted on whatever was left of the kill. I approached the pile of flints and bones, knelt and picked up something myself.

It was a piece of jawbone. That much was obvious by the curve, the sockets, and the single gleaming canine that emerged from its cracked and brittle depths.

"Tooth of the tiger," I said softly.

"They're all gone, Nestor," Isabelle said softly, staring at it in sad fascination.

"Not all," said Julie. She beckoned us to follow to the far wall of the cave where Waku sat cross-legged, nose to nose with a Tasmanian tiger.

It was a brilliant portrait. Even after thousands of years, the colors were as vibrant and alive as the day the aboriginal painter had smeared them lovingly across the rock. The rendition was crude—at least compared to the fine drawings I had purchased at Salamanca Place—but it contained a certain life and soul that the more precise Western images lacked. We stood in front of it for a long time.

"Do you believe there are any left, Julie?" Isabelle asked quietly.

"I know there are."

"You've seen them?" Waku asked sharply.

She hesitated. "I've seen something."

"But not definitely a tiger?" Waku pursued.

"Definitely something the size and power of a tiger."

"If you didn't actually see it, how do you know it was a tiger?" I asked.

"Why haven't you claimed the reward?" Isabelle added.

"I knew by the smell, Mister Dark. The smell. As for the reward, there are more important things to me than Japanese money. I do not want those people here. I want to protect this land, not contribute to its rape by foreign hunters with fancy guns and shiny watches and satellites and computers."

"Did you know Joel Tinker?" I asked her.

"I knew of him."

"Do you believe he found the tiger?"

"I believe it would be hard for a white man to do. Local people know of the reward and have come up with nothing."

"Joel specialized in the hard to do," I said.

When we got back to the river, Isabelle watched from the bank while the rest of us made a human bridge and unloaded the tiny submarine from the Cessna's cargo compartment. Julie watched from the bank while I took care of the small things that always ruin a good plan. It took me a little time to set the aft batteries up properly, as they had leaked from the buffeting and the altitude. I capped them, wiped them down, and checked the circuitry with the built-in pattern tester. Then I attached the nose section, ran my fingers over all the "O" ring seals to ensure they were properly seated, and greased them. I checked for any loose wires to the motors, and rocked the circuit boards back and forth with my fingers in their settings to make certain nothing had rattled loose.

Finally I set the video camera in the conning tower, verifying the position of the mirrors that reflected the light gathered through the thimble-sized periscope down to the camera lens. I told Waku to hold his hands up, got down on my hands and knees, and checked that the input was rightside up and in focus from ten feet to infinity. I sealed the sub and set it carefully on the surface of the water.

"We're miles from anywhere. Are you just going to let it go until the batteries run dry and it sinks?" Julie asked.

"The batteries won't run dry. It's going to sail *with* the flow of the river, not against it. I've programmed it for time and speed using a map, and set the deflectors to keep it off the riverbanks. It will just float out to the mouth of the harbor."

"That could take days!" said Julie.

"I certainly hope so, but the camera will only run at night."

"And tigers are supposed to be nocturnal," Julie breathed.

"What happens when it gets to the harbor?" asked Waku.

I dug a flat receiving panel out of my pocket and held it up. "It will surface, shut down, and send out a beacon. We'll go pick it up."

We watched the tiny boat bob in the river for a moment, as if it were considering what to do.

"It looks like a little coffin," said Isabelle.

The submarine maneuvered silently to the middle of the river, turned so that its nose pointed perfectly downstream, and submerged, leaving only a tiny gleaming eye above the lapping waves. I glanced around and noticed that the four of us were standing rigidly, like attentive mourners at a military funeral. I thought of Joel.

The weather on the return trip was calmer, but the wind had picked up over the harbor, making our landing far rougher than our takeoff. The metal struts that ran diagonally from the center of the pilot console out to the leading edge of the overhead wings shuddered noticeably as the pontoons hit water.

Upon our return to Macquarie House, I noticed a pearl-white Nissan 300 ZK sports car parked next to my battered Fairlane. The car caught my eye because it seemed so utterly out of place on an island which took a scant four hours to cross in a pickup truck, and where the highest reasonable speed on the poorly engineered, ungraded roads wasn't much more than seventy miles an hour.

"Unbridled excess," Julie observed. Waku made a point of caressing the car's fender as we passed it on our way into the inn.

A tiny Japanese man was lounging in the reception area. He wore a Gucci tie, Lanvin shirt, and a Hong Kong suit. His skin, particularly around the creases of his neck, was smooth and polished as marble and he stank of Aramis cologne. He uncrossed his legs and stood as we came through the door.

"Mr. Dark? My name is Nozawa. I have been looking forward to meeting you." He worked hard to keep what was obviously a high voice low and the result was strangled, like an adolescent afraid to let his old tones through.

Isabelle froze, watching me. Julie Iringili seemed distant and amused. Waku physically bristled. I put a restraining hand on his shoulder.

"Do we have friends in common?"

"I do not believe that we do. I represent a group in Tokyo interested in Dr. Tinker's final notes. Do you have them?"

"Maybe."

"Come now, Mr. Dark, let's not play games. Dr. Tinker was in touch with me. I know that he had located at least one living example of the thylacine. When I learned of his death and your arrival. . . ."

"Lieutenant Pennington?" I interjected.

He smiled. "I thought perhaps we could work something out."

"I haven't run across any tigers," I said evenly.

"But you do have the notes?"

"Some Japanese men tried to kill me the other night."

"I'm glad to see they were unsuccessful," he replied.

"Six million dollars," I said.

"Actually, Mr. Dark, the reward is five million."

"Not *your* reward. *Mine.* The Dark Foundation is offering six million American dollars for a live Tasmanian tiger."

His already pale face faded a shade.

# Chapter 12

LONG BEFORE I was a SWAT sniper, and long before I ended Waku's career as an informant, I used to go places with my Uncle Andrew and meet the men who ruled the world. These were, I learned, mostly quiet men with unpronounceable names who wore quiet ties. Uncle Andrew referred to them as "dealmakers," and when I asked him what that meant, he told me that they helped people to do things they both wanted to do and then took some of the money. When I asked what a third person could add to a deal wherein two people knew what it was they wanted, he answered me with a single word:

"Balls."

So it was with Arnet Pichaud, one of the first and certainly always the most exalted of my uncle's dealmaker friends. Secretly, always secretly, Pichaud advised presidents and prime ministers and chief executive officers. His name was never mentioned, at least in financial or geopolitical circles, and he lived in a Manhattan triplex whose front door was a fake fire hose cabinet. If there was big money attached, Arnet knew all there was to know. When Andrew Dark died, Arnet was at the funeral, and he toasted him, quietly, first as his close friend, second as the world's greatest dealmaker.

When Isabelle failed to get the necessary information on the Japanese from Rignola, I decided to try Pichaud. After the confrontation with Nozawa, I went up to my room in the inn and placed the transoceanic call.

"Mr. Pichaud is abroad," his secretary informed me over the telephone. "Who shall I tell him called?"

"Nestor Dark."

"Forgive me—I didn't recognize you, Mr. Dark."

"I'm calling from Australia."

"Do you have instructions for me?"

"Only to have him call me."

"But he's in Australia, too. At a conference in Sydney."

"A conference?" I doubted that Arnet Pichaud had ever attended a conference in his life. He hated crowds, and he worked his deals solo.

"Well, that's what he told me."

"Where is he staying?"

"The Intercontinental Sydney."

I hung up and reached the New South Wales operator. She rang me through to the hotel. When I asked for his room, I was greeted by a long pause.

"We have nobody by that name registered at the hotel, sir," the clerk told me over the crackling line.

"I need to leave a message for that nobody," I said.

The clerk took the message without confirming or denying that he would pass it on.

"We have to wait," I said.

"That's awful," Isabelle answered, unbuttoning my shirt from behind and leaning her thick crown of blonde hair across my shoulder, so that her hot breath sprayed my chest.

"He's going to call any minute," I managed, my voice clogging as she leaned over and dove deeper.

"You don't know that. You don't even know if he's there," she whispered.

She shucked herself out of her blue jeans, smelling of the river, and climbed over me so that one smooth thigh was pressed against my chest. The phone rang, and she sighed a long one and flopped onto the bed.

It was Pichaud.

"What the hell are you doing Down Under?" he boomed. He was a small man, but he had a big voice.

"I should ask you the same question."

"But I'm not in Tasmania, dear boy."

"A friend died. I'm here to find out why. I need your help."

"You always do."

"I've met a man named Nozawa today. He represents what he claims is a cartel of wealthy Japanese interested in procuring a supposedly extinct animal called the Tasmanian tiger. They're offering five million dollars. I think his group murdered my friend and shot at me."

"I hope you've upped the ante."

"Six million. Great minds think alike."

"So now you want to know who they are and the real reason they're putting up the money?"

"Can you help?"

"It will take a day or two."

"Isabelle and I will fly over."

"She's with you in Tasmania?"

"Right here on the bed."

"Really, you're not so different from your uncle after all. I'll book you the suite next to mine."

It rained again that night, and Nozawa was absent from the dinner table. Graham Pullman told me he had gone to try another restaurant in town. Julie and Waku were poor conversationalists during the meal, spending most of their time trading cow eyes and tasting food off one another's plate. The air was thick with electricity from the storm, and even Divac seemed in a testy mood. He served me a soufflé of puréed potato and spinach that was in every way the equal of his morning effort. The house creaked and groaned with the ozone and the wind. Isabelle shivered at the sounds, and picked idly at her roast pheasant in pink cracked pepper sauce.

"House is haunted, so don't worry," Pullman laughed.

"Nestor's home in Connecticut is haunted, but I've never felt uncomfortable there," said Isabelle.

"I hope you don't feel that way here, Miss Redfield, but the truth is, Tasmania was one enormous prison full of souls tortured and abandoned far from home. They stay here now, part of the island," Pullman explained.

"In this house?" asked Isabelle.

"Among many others. If it's over a hundred years old, you can expect to find someone without a flesh and blood body within its walls," said Pullman.

Divac was serving some fresh-baked bread during the discourse.

"You might feel a light pressure on the chest or have a conversation with a soldier named Philip who grumbles about the rations," he said, looking directly at Isabelle.

"Well, he certainly wouldn't grumble about tonight's rations," I said, looking at Isabelle's expression and trying to lighten things up.

Later I lay in bed with the reading light on and Isabelle snuggled close against me, Joel Tinker's papers on my chest.

"Myths are really important," she announced, staring at the ceiling.

I mumbled something, caught up in Tinker's passionate description of the Tasmanian heartland and the thrill of the hunt.

"Are you listening to me?"

"I smelled the tiger today," I read. "It was a rancid smell, muskier than kangaroo, like blood and mushrooms mixed together. It made me plunge headlong into the forest in pursuit, even though it was night and I scratched myself on brambles."

"He was chasing the myth," Isabelle said.

"I never knew Joel was so emotional," I murmured, leafing through the pages more rapidly.

"Don't you see, Nestor? That's what I've been trying to tell you. We all have those feelings inside of us. That's why we make up myths."

"The tiger is no myth," I said. "It's a real animal."

"It *was* a real animal. It's as dead and gone as the dinosaurs."

"The dinosaurs lived millions of years ago," I protested.

She rose on her elbow and faced me with a skeptical look.

"And people still write about them, and talk about them, and make movies about them, hoping to find them in a land that time forgot. They still capture our imagination. People still fantasize about traveling back in a time machine to see one. I know I would. I bet you would, too. One year dead, or thirty million years dead, it's all the same.''

"Not if they still exist," I reasoned.

"The tiger is a myth. Myths are dreams people can share. It got hold of Joel Tinker, and it's gotten hold of you."

I read some more of Tinker's notes, then laid them on the bedside table.

"I think you're wrong. I don't think the thylacine is a myth. I think it's real. These notes weren't written millions of years ago. They were written in the last couple of weeks. If Joel Tinker says he saw a Tasmanian tiger, it's no myth to me.''

She sighed, smiled, turned on the electric blanket.

"Forget that. I'll keep you warm," I said, switching it off.

So I rolled to face her, kissed her hair, her neck, her lips, then lower. She sighed, pulled me to her, threw her head back.

"You're just a boy with a dream," she murmured.

Instead of tapering off as it had on previous nights, the rain grew heavier, tapping a roar on the skylight. The gale picked up too, rattling the windows in their frames. At 3:00 A.M. I opened my eyes, awakened by the storm. Isabelle was fast asleep, her hands clasping the pillow as if in prayer, her blonde ringlets framing her face like an angel's halo. I couldn't see much beyond her, because the storm clouds hid the moon and the stars, leaving only a little reflected light from the welcome lamp at the front of the house.

I became aware that there was someone else in the room. I looked around, imagining a string of kung fu moves in my mind, preparing for an attack from any direction, but reluctant to leave the false security of the covers and Isabelle's radiant warmth. The air in the room was cold.

And Uncle Andrew was at the foot of the bed.

He was floating, lower than the ceiling, but not quite rooted in the ground. He wore the old blue cardigan he'd died in—cashmere, of course, with small black buttons.

"Unk," I said.

He smiled sadly, floating a bit higher, then settling down. His face grew more and less distinct, pulsing like a giant blood vessel.

"Why don't you think of me?" he asked.

I sat bolt upright in bed.

"I think of you all the time!"

He shook his head, still smiling sadly.

"Not anymore. You used to, but not anymore."

"You're wrong. You're always with me."

"My doing, not yours," he said.

"I'm aware of you all the time. Surrounded by you all the time. By your life. Your things."

"My things. Like my Rolls Royce?"

I felt an anxious pang in my stomach, like before an exam, like being caught red handed.

"I didn't think you'd mind about the Rolls. You told me you never liked it anyway. Told me it made you feel like an old man," I said desperately.

"It did."

"Where are you?

"Here with you."

"Are you in heaven?"

He shook his head, still smiling the sad smile, like he was talking to a child who just didn't get it.

"Hell?" I barely managed to whisper.

He shook his head again.

"You don't think of me enough, Nestor."

"But I do. All the time. I live your life."

"Not my life. I wouldn't chase a tiger."

"I owe you everything."

"You don't owe me anything, Nestor. I just want you to think about me. Will you promise to do that?"

"I promise," I said. I started to cry then, suddenly realizing that he was going away. He grew fainter, and I held out my hand.

"Will you come to see me again?"

"It's difficult," he said softly. I reached out my hand even further. I couldn't seem to make myself get up and go to him. I couldn't control my body that much. He reached his hand toward me, too. We stretched towards each other. I wanted so badly to touch him my fingertips ached.

Then I could only make out his upper half. Then I could only make out his face. Then a few wisps of his hair.

Then he was gone.

# Chapter 13

I WAS STILL crying when the sun came up. I ran a shower and turned up the heat as far as it would go. I stood with my head against the tile until the water was as cold as the Tasman sea. Isabelle appeared, a flesh-colored apparition through the frosted glass of the shower door. She stuck her head in. I turned away.

"Jesus, it's cold, Nestor. You should have woken me up. I'm much better than a cold shower."

I kept my face away from her until finally she cupped me under the chin and swiveled me around.

"Good God, what's wrong?" she whispered, staring at my swollen eyes.

Her voice pierced my numb world. I wanted to answer, but I couldn't speak. I was too dead inside.

"Are you sick?"

I shook my head. The hard shower pounded my cheeks like nails.

"Uncle Andrew came to see me last night," I managed at last. My voice sounded distant and tinny and not like me at all.

"A bad dream?"

"It wasn't a dream."

She leaned over and turned off the water. I stood shivering until she wrapped me in a bath towel and climbed into the damp stall with me, holding me hard against her.

"Why didn't you wake me?" she whispered.

"It happened too fast. It was just about him and me."

"What did he want?"

"He made me promise to think of him more often."

"You think about him all the time," Isabelle caressed my head.

"He was mad I sold the Rolls Royce."

"You told me he hated that car."

"I thought he did."

"You sure this wasn't a guilty dream, Nestor? It seems funny that Andrew Dark's ghost would want to talk about a car."

"He wasn't in heaven and he wasn't in hell," I said.

"Maybe he's nowhere at all unless you think about him. Maybe that's what the visit was all about," she said thoughtfully.

"I never believed in an afterlife before," I said, feeling the tears well up again.

"Are you relieved?"

"He told me he would never chase a tiger."

"You're not him, Nestor. Sometimes I think you forget that."

\* \* \*

*Wall Street Journal* editor Sam Houser and I had met over Andrew Dark's obituary. He did an accurate job, kinder than some would have, and I told him I owed him one. Some years later I paid back the debt by giving him the scoop on a major counterfeiting operation. While I packed an overnight bag for Sydney, Isabelle called Sam from our room at Macquarie House and gave him news of my six million dollar reward.

"He wants to talk to you," Isabelle whispered, her hand over the telephone.

I shook my head. I was too dry-mouthed and exhausted from the previous night to talk to the press.

Isabelle extracted a promise to publish the reward story while I slipped Joel Tinker's papers into a compartment in the false lid of the weapons case and set the intrusion monitor located at the rear lip.

Julie Iringili offered us a floatplane ride to Devonport, the nearest airport that offered a flight to Sydney. But I declined, and we set off in the Fairlane.

The trip took us up the Murchison Highway toward Burnie, and industrial town on the beach some twenty miles from Devonport. This route—the only one possible—cut off the northwest corner of the island.

"What's up there?" Isabelle asked, pointing at the blank section on the map.

"Mountains and rivers," I answered. I knew I wasn't being very good company, but I still felt hollow and quiet from the night.

"That's a lot of land without roads. Maybe there are tigers there."

"I thought you said tigers went out with the dinosaurs," I answered.

She smiled, but my mind was as blank as the uncharted area on the map, and I couldn't bring myself to smile back. I stayed mute all the way to the plane.

Connections to Sydney were smooth, and by the time we landed there, I was beginning to feel better. Arnet's driver was waiting for us in the arrival lobby. He gave Isabelle an appreciative once-over and whisked us without incident to the Hotel Intercontinental. Arnet had left a message at the desk, asking us to meet him in the rooftop restaurant.

While Isabelle freshened up, I took in the magnificent view of Circular Quay, the famous opera house, and the harbor offered by the picture window in our suite.

"Hard to believe this is the same country as Tasmania," Isabelle observed, appearing next to me and looking at the endless stretch of protected water.

"It's not, really. Tasmania is a part of Australia, but from what I've seen the only link is political. We might as well be on another planet."

Sydney's dress code exceeded Strahan's, so we rode the elevator to the penthouse restaurant dressed in high style, me in a knife-creased square cut British suit, Isabelle in a sprayed-on passionfruit-colored cocktail dress. Arnet was sitting at the bar, dressed in a linen safari suit, a handkerchief around his throat.

"Nobody dresses like that anymore," I said.

"Nice to see you, too," he answered sardonically, toasting me with a glass of fine port.

"Ah, the life of leisure. Port in the afternoon," I said.

"How do you put up with this snotty shit?" he asked Isabelle, standing and bringing her hand to his mouth.

"He has his good points."

"The only one I know is you," Pichaud replied.

We took a table by a window which offered the same view as we had from the suite, only higher and broader. Perched like hawks, we watched ferries go back and forth between the north side beaches and Circular Quay. Arnet and Isabelle feasted on Moreton Bay bugs, a popular dish of sautéed Australian crayfish. I had steamed vegetables.

"You still jet-lagged?" I asked Arnet.

"Jet lag is for pussies," he said.

"I want to take Isabelle to the zoo. Will you go with us?"

"The zoo!"

"Taronga. I hear it's a great one."

"No Tasmanian tigers, though. They're gone with the dinosaurs," said Isabelle.

"I wouldn't have thought you'd be in favor of zoos, Nestor," said Arnet.

"They have two great missions. One to educate the public, another as a repository of endangered species whose homes we're wrecking. I'm in favor of any zoo that performs one or both of these tasks well."

Arnet studied the dessert menu, desperately trying to think of a reason why he couldn't spend the afternoon at the monkey house.

"We can take a ferry over. Get on, get off," Isabelle suggested.

"Arnet doesn't like to go anywhere foreign without a bodyguard. He's afraid of being kidnapped and held for ransom. He doesn't realize he's the one with the money. Nobody would pay."

"He has you to protect him," said Isabelle.

"All right, all right, stop treating me like I'm not here. I'll go with you to the zoo. I have no meetings this afternoon anyway," Arnet announced.

"You really know how to make friends warm and fuzzy inside," I said.

It was hot on the ferry, and we stayed aft, under the awning but still in the wind.

"The Japanese have a long history of trophy hunting. They're famous for it," Arnet began.

"They're environmental pirates. They collect elephant tusk, rhino horn, bits and pieces of the innards of endangered species. They still kill whales, for God's sake," I said.

"For their own sake, not God's. To enhance their sex lives and make them live longer," said Arnet.

The ferry drew up to her mooring. Fighting the heat, we climbed the stairs to the entrance, where I bought three tickets and we entered the zoo.

"I'm convinced that whoever is behind the tiger money thought they could avoid paying up by killing Joel Tinker and stealing his information," I said.

"So you believe it's the Japanese, and they believe you have Tinker's notes," Pichaud mused.

"I do. Any idea who's behind the money?" I asked.

"Look!" Isabelle cried, delighted by the sight of a magnificent pair of giant black-and-red birds, their heads crowned by frond-like crests.

"Black palm cockatoos," Arnet announced calmly. "The rarest of the southern hemisphere parrots."

"I had no idea you were a bird-watcher," I said, amazed.

"I was a member of the Royal Ornithological Society before your first night with a hooker," he sniffed.

Isabelle slapped him on the arm.

"Let's stop talking about chicks and start talking about tigers," she said.

"Nectar feeders. Awfully messy in the aviary," said Arnet, stopping to peer into a cage full of brilliantly colored South Pacific rainbow lories.

"Tigers!" Isabelle warned.

"There's a fellow called Kimura. He has the largest collection of rare and endangered species in Japan. Purports to breed them, but really just likes to keep count. One-up the neighbors, that sort of thing. I learned about him when he imported a large colony of marabou storks to his estate near Tokyo. They died, of course. They need carrion, you see. He wouldn't feed them anything dead, so he lost them."

"Does he have anything to do with canned hunts?" asked Isabelle.

I had never heard the term and said so.

"Trophy hunters love to do their own shooting, even if it's in a barrel. You can't shoot a black panther or a blackbuck antelope or an axis deer in the wild, but you can if it's been captive bred and privately sold," Arnet explained with disgust.

"People pay to shoot them in a fenced-in yard, or even right in the cage, then mount them on the wall," said Isabelle.

"Big cats are especially popular," Arnet said.

"You think someone would pay to shoot a captive thylacine?" I asked in disbelief.

"Tens of thousands," said Isabelle.

"Hundreds of thousands," said Arnet.

"You think Kimura wants the tiger for someone else to shoot?"

"He probably just wants it for himself, but he's not the kind of guy to turn down a profitable venture, either," said Arnet.

"So you think he's the man behind the five million?" I asked.

"If he isn't, he'll know who is."

"Does he know your name?"

Arnet Pichaud withered me with a look.

"You want to meet him, you'll have to go to Japan."

Isabelle exclaimed again, as this time we arrived at the mammal house. A billboard explained that Australian mammals, known as marsupials, carried their young in pouches as they developed. There was a duckbilled platypus on exhibit, as well as an echidna, both monotremes, or egg-laying mammals. There was a Tasmanian devil, too, a wolverine-sized predator from the island we had just left.

And there was an empty cage, clean and neat and well laid out, with a cardboard cutout of a thylacine and a written explanation of its recent extinction. The three of us stood together while Isabelle read it aloud. She had tears in her eyes when she finished.

"Kimura." Arnet Pichaud nodded absently, staring at the striped, dog-sized rendition.

"I don't have any clothes for Japan," Isabelle said faintly.

"You can buy some in Tokyo," I said.

"But the dollar is weak, Nestor. It'll be so expensive."

"Pleading poverty doesn't become you," Arnet observed.

# Chapter 14

THAT NIGHT ARNET'S driver took us back to Sydney airport for the 10:30 P.M. Qantas flight to Narita, Japan. We settled into our first class seats and watched Billy Crystal's *City Slickers*. It was shown in dubbed Japanese with stilted English subtitles. Isabelle tried for an explanation of why they hadn't simply titled the movie in Japanese, or at least used the real dialogue in the English titles. In response, the stewardess assured her that Japanese people loved cowboy movies.

I slept hard after the movie, awakening to the sound of Isabelle breaking the fast with a sushi roll. I groaned and turned away. She plopped an apple and the *Wall Street Journal* in my lap.

"Sam Houser came through," she said.

I gave the article a cursory, yawning look.

"I don't know which of us sounds like the bigger monster, me or the thylacine. I come across bored and depraved, like a man with money to burn," I said in disgust.

"You're not bored," she stroked my face.

"Well this should get Kimura's attention, anyway," I announced. I tossed the paper to my feet and went back to sleep.

Isabelle suggested renting a car as we waited for our bags at Narita, but before we could make it to the rental counters, we were approached by a driver carrying a white card with my name written on it. I identified myself to him.

"A great pleasure to meet you, Mr. Dark. I am Ikura. Kimura-*sama* sent me to bring you to his home." He looked no more than seventeen years old, slim, with a long neck and hands and a perfectly fitted black chauffeur's uniform.

"I have nothing to wear," Isabelle said immediately.

"We need clothing," I said. "This is an unexpected trip."

"Kimura-*sama* is expecting you for lunch," Ikura glanced nervously at his wristwatch.

"I don't care what he's expecting. I need to do some shopping," said Isabelle.

"It will have to be dinner. Ms. Redfield needs clothing," I said.

"Kimura-*sama* has plenty of clothes."

"I buy my own, thank you. Take us downtown to the Ginza, please," Isabelle commanded.

Ikura looked at me imploringly.

"We'd better go to the Ginza," I said.

Isabelle was transfixed by the urban landscape as Ikura cut and thrust through the city's seething masses.

"No wonder they're buying up Australia. You can't

turn around without bumping into somebody. What a contrast to Tasmania,'' said Isabelle.

"They're buying America, too,'' I answered, keeping my eye on the densely polluted horizon.

At every intersection, and often in between, an army of sweepers and wipers was working to keep the city clean.

I pointed out a mountain of disposable plastic containers piled in one corner waiting for pick-up.

"What waste!'' said Isabelle.

"Aesthetically they're very advanced people, but environmentally they're pigs,'' I said.

"Everybody is an environmental pig to you,'' she answered.

Ikura recommended the Mitsukoshi department store, claiming that even the emperor bought his underwear there. I was satisfied to pick up a few changes of clothing, but Isabelle insisted upon trying out several boutiques, balking at the prices and buying things anyway, returning often to the car to leave her goods and start again. Ikura grew more agitated by the minute.

Despite being a world center, Tokyo proved insufficiently cosmopolitan to take Isabelle Redfield in stride. Courteous and efficient clerks brought her shoes and jumpsuits and scarves without batting an eye, but young Japanese schoolgirls looked through the store windows at her crown of golden hair, pointing and covering their giggles and teeth. Some even came in and wanted to touch her. The men checked her out too, without ever looking her in the eye.

"Admit it. You like the gawking,'' she said.

"Don't be silly.''

"You do! I know you do!''

I ignored her and pointed out the video wall across

the street, where hundreds of monitor-quality television screens, fed by a video camera aimed squarely
at the street, were synchronized to provide a gigantic
image. Isabelle wandered idly about, squinting upwards at the buildings, looking for the camera, until
suddenly her image appeared, filling the wall with
blonde hair. The sidewalk was instantly abuzz, Isabelle wailed, and we ran for the shelter of Kimura's
limousine.

Clothed and equipped for our visit with the eccen-
tric Japanese millionaire who had summoned us, we
relaxed in the back of the limousine while Ikura drove
the expressway through Saitama and Tochigi prefec-
tures. We headed into Fukushima, the nose of the car
aimed right at the five-thousand-foot peak of Mt.
Bandai.

"This blew up from steam in eighteen eighty-eight.
There were the Hibara and Nagase rivers. Now there
are lakes of many colors from the copper and other
minerals," Ikura explained, gesturing at the ragged
mountaintop before us.

"Are we almost there?" asked Isabelle.

Ikura nodded.

"Mr. Kimura lives near the mountain?" I asked.

"You will see."

Kimura's estate was on Onogawa-ko, one of the
three largest lakes created by the eruption a century
before. The house was long and low, made from native woods to blend in beautifully with the lakefront,
streams, and forest. It was a home worthy of Andrew
Dark.

"I didn't expect something like this. It shows such
sensitivity to nature," Isabelle murmured.

Ikura pulled the big black limousine to the front door of the house, and we walked together through perfectly symmetrical plantings, Ikura at our side, laden down with stacks of shopping bags so high they knocked against his hat.

Kimura was waiting just inside. He could have been anywhere from thirty-five to fifty-five, thick but not fat, like a *sumo* wrestler on a liquid diet. His bow was deep and his hand was hard. Unlike the men in Tokyo, he looked Isabelle in the eye.

"Thank you for the lift," I said, bowing.

"Thank you for honoring my car and driver," he responded.

"I assume that you spoke with Arnet Pichaud?"

"Not directly. Mr. Pichaud and I have never actually met. There are people between us."

He waved his hand, and we followed him into a luxurious living area with low, hardwood furniture looking out over a central atrium filled with an exquisite rock garden. Ikura disappeared with our bags.

"Are these friends also interested in exotic animals?" I asked.

Kimura studied me with curiosity for a moment, as if I were a specimen under a dissecting scope.

"Do you collect nothing, Mr. Dark?"

"I have a few toys."

"What sort of toys?"

"Remote control planes and boats and cars. A small model railroad set."

". . . and an Aston Martin Virage, a hot-rod Ford sedan, a couple of interesting motorcycles, one of the most highly advanced turboprops in the world," Kimura finished.

Isabelle paled visibly.

"How did you . . . ?" she sputtered.

"You forgot the guns," I said, trying to duplicate his icy calm.

Kimura smiled and walked to a tall cabinet crafted from a tropical hardwood I did not recognize.

"What lovely wood," said Isabelle.

"Purple heart," said Kimura as he opened the double doors to reveal a rack of expensive rifles. He pulled one out, opened the bolt and tossed it to me. I caught it with one hand, my eyes still on him.

"Exotic," I said.

"I'm disappointed you don't recognize it," he smiled.

"Heym SR-20 Trophy," I replied.

The smile disappeared from his face.

He tossed another one and I caught it with my free hand.

"Anschutz fifteen sixteen D," I said with barely a glance.

I propped the rifles against the back of a chair as I saw him reaching for another one.

"Steyr Mannlicher Luxus," I said as it came sailing across the room.

My eyes were still trained on Kimura, but I felt Isabelle's smile in my heart. She hated guns, but I was making her proud.

"Perhaps tomorrow we can shoot," he suggested.

"Perhaps tomorrow we can. And Ms. Redfield and I would love to see your animals."

Our bedroom was furnished as beautifully as the rest of the house, with a glass-framed door overlooking the perfect rock garden. A small stone footpath led from just outside the room to a steaming hot tub. Isabelle organized her purchases while I tried to talk her into a soak.

"The art of bathing is perfected here. It's a treat you can't miss."

"And how would you know? Did you stop here after your uncle died on your new-millionaire world tour?"

As if on cue, a beautiful, smooth-skinned young girl, her body wrapped in a kimono and the bun of her hair secured by wood sticks, appeared at the atrium door.

"You will have bath now, yes?" she said, looking straight at me.

"Wait just one minute," said Isabelle.

"Lady too?" a second, taller girl appeared.

"I don't like this," said Isabelle.

"You don't mind when I lick sauterne-soaked raspberries off your bare stomach, so why does a hot bath bother you?"

"I don't know these people," she hissed.

The taller girl reached for Isabelle and led her gently by the hand out into the garden and the tub.

I hadn't noticed the shower head because it was artfully concealed by a twist of creeping vine. The tall girl helped Isabelle off with her clothes and the shorter girl removed mine. I watched Isabelle carefully, but the girls were as deliberate as nurses and as gentle as lovers. Before long we were soaped up and rinsed off and ready for the tub.

The water was hot enough to turn toenails to gelatin. Isabelle winced when she put her foot in.

"It dilates the pores and relaxes the muscles," I said.

"I don't trust Kimura, and I don't feel *comfortable* here," Isabelle whispered.

The girls were as fascinated by Isabelle's blonde hair as the children downtown had been, but they tried not to show it. They took rough brushes and began to scrub our heads, necks, backs, holding our arms out with gentle guiding motions, positioning them so they stayed just as sure as if they had been planted. I saw Isabelle close her eyes right before I closed mine.

Isabelle was silent as we dressed for dinner.

"You're mad at yourself for liking it, aren't you?" I asked softly.

"Japan is a terrible place for women," she answered.

"I didn't get the impression those girls were unhappy."

"They weren't girls, they were women."

"They were under twenty-one. That makes them girls. Happy girls, at that."

"They're only happy because they don't know any better."

"Are you happy?"

She shifted in her dress, straightening her shoulders, and looked at me.

"Sometimes."

"So who are you to judge them?"

"I'm not judging them, Nestor, I'm telling you I think it's a shame that they bathe people for a living."

"Wouldn't you bathe *them?*"

"Certainly not. Would you?"

"Sure," I smiled.

She threw a pillow at me, hard.

"Wrong answer, buddy boy."

Kimura sat across from us, his legs in lotus position, his belly pushing against the low table.

"How did you enjoy your visit to Tasmania?" he inquired.

"Very much," I replied.

A young man whom we had not seen before appeared with a plate of steaming eggplant and other mountain vegetables. He placed them in front of me. Isabelle and our host ate an elaborately prepared fish.

"How long have you been a vegetarian?"

"He eats *sushi* every once in a while," said Isabelle.

"Can we talk about the tiger? I understand you are responsible for the five million dollar reward."

Kimura held up his hand.

"Business tomorrow, pleasure tonight. Did you enjoy your bath?"

Isabelle clenched her teeth.

"It was perfect," I responded.

He watched me maneuver my pointed chopsticks around a slice of something orange.

"Mountain yam," he said. "High in beta carotene. Good for the body. Fights cancer."

"Anything good for the body in a dead tiger?" Isabelle asked.

"Perhaps tomorrow, while you and I shoot rifles, Ikura can take Ms. Redfield for a tour of the lakes," Kimura said to me.

"You can ignore your *geisha* girls, but you can't ignore me," Isabelle said furiously. I kicked her under the table.

"It is a Japanese custom to ignore rude guests," Kimura smiled pleasantly.

She fled the table in a flurry, and I followed her, leaving the luscious yams behind.

# Chapter 15

THE SHEETS BETWEEN us grew cold that night, and I rose early. While Isabelle slept, I dressed in sweat clothes and went out to greet the sunbeams piercing the veil of mist above Lake Onogawa-ko. The air was cold, and there was a light frost on Kimura's lawn.

I began my morning workout with a series of moves from the *Wing Chun* system of Chinese boxing. These entailed bringing the elbows to the much-vaunted "center," that mental and physical construct which serves the fighter by aligning him properly for an offensive strike while simultaneously helping him guard his vitals. I had not worked out in several days, and my tight shoulder joints popped and clicked in protest as I angled my elbows down and extended first the upward *bong sau* block and then the outward *tan sau*. I worked my upper body for half an hour, then began deep legwork from the White Crane system, rocking from one leg to the other and extending my toes to imitate the bird. I felt my hips slowly give in to the new day, and with that giving, a release of tension. Kimura appeared about then.

He was dressed in gaudy sports clothes, and carried one of the previous night's bolt-action rifles in each hand.

*"Tai chi?"* he asked.

"Just some exercises," I answered.

I don't perform martial arts in front of others, and I don't like to discuss my abilities, especially with potential foes. I was annoyed at Kimura for having discovered me at work, and even more annoyed at myself for having let him.

"Ready to shoot?" he asked.

"I was born ready."

He smiled and held out both rifles. I took the Anschutz.

He led me away from the lake and into the woods alongside his house. He had set up a formal target range there, with the hill as a backstop and moveable target frames on posts which could be put in holes in the ground marked at Olympic intervals. I got the feel of the Anschutz trigger while he set two frames at 100 meters and tacked paper.

He watched me as I brought the barrel up to my left eye and gazed through the sights.

"You are a very unusual man, Mr. Dark," he observed. "I don't know many left-eyed marksman."

"Seems to work all right," I answered.

"Best of five shots?"

"I don't compete without a prize," I said.

"I have nothing to offer you but my home."

I lowered the muzzle.

"I've already enjoyed that. It's time for bigger and better things. I want to see your animals. No animals, no shooting."

"You are so American," he answered.

"And proud of it. You shoot first," I ordered.

"Please. I'm sure I have much to learn from a police sniper. I wouldn't dream of shooting first," he smiled.

"That makes two of us," I replied evenly, lowering the muzzle.

"A standoff," Kimura clapped in apparent delight.

"We'll take turns," I said. "You shoot the first round."

He raised his Steyr casually and released a .308 slug without appearing to aim at all. I looked at the hole through the spotting scope. It was half an inch shy of the center of the bull's-eye.

"Very good," I said, raising the Anschutz and moving the bolt to chamber a round.

I set the target on top of the "V" and let out my breath just as Kimura spoke.

"I knew your uncle," he said.

My shot went wild, hitting the seven ring at about four o'clock.

"Ten years ago we accomplished the buy-out of a Korean pharmaceutical company together," he continued.

"I don't recall hearing about it."

"We sold it right away."

"For a substantial profit, no doubt."

"We shared an interest in making money. I was sorry to hear of his painful death."

"Did you have Dr. Tinker killed?" I asked suddenly.

Kimura ignored the question and raised the Steyr again, taking more careful aim this time, as if dissatisfied by the fact that the last round had not been geometrically perfect. I watched his finger tighten almost imperceptibly around the sporter's trigger, waiting patiently for the perfect moment.

"I have Joel Tinker's map. If you send more men, I'll kill them too," I said.

Kimura twitched hard enough to send the bullet into the five ring.

He went silently to the scope, then turned to me, fighting for self-control.

"Perhaps we should agree to end the conversation until after the shooting," he said tightly.

His remaining three shots were bull's-eyes, as were mine. I beat him by two points.

"The animals," I demanded.

Of all the animals in Kimura's collection, the reptiles surprised me most. They included dusk-colored tuataras from the New Zealand archipelago and brilliant Fiji iguanas, radiated tortoises from Madagascar and white-and-caramel albino pythons from Burma. All were immaculately kept in a heated, separate building some hundred yards from the house. Kimura showed us the elaborate climate-control system and the backup generators.

"Mr. Dark is quite a marksman," he told Isabelle.

"Nestor had a hand in saving some snakes," she replied, staring at two pythons.

"Rock rattlers from the Southwest," I demurred. "It was a real estate deal."

Kimura took us to see the birds next. Like his herpetarium, his aviary was climate-controlled and immaculately maintained. There were endangered Puerto Rican Amazon parrots there, a pair of slender-billed cockatoos, and an extensive collection of hummingbirds.

The last section of his private collection contained

only bears, and it was of these that Kimura was most obviously proud.

"The Malayan sun bear," he introduced.

Out of doors, the musky odor was intense. Indoors it would have been overpowering. The bears were far more active than any I had ever seen in a public zoo, prowling their deep pit purposefully, eyes aglint at the prospect of combat, victory, blood, and repast.

"You let them loose so your friends can hunt them?" asked Isabelle sarcastically.

Kimura turned crimson.

"My friends do not hunt captive animals," he replied.

"No shooting bears in the cage, eh? Then what about eating the gall bladder?"

"What's going on here?" I asked, physically interposing myself between Isabelle and a glowering Kimura.

"Japanese men think bear bladders make them better lovers," she answered, still challenging Kimura with her eyes.

"We are not savages, Ms. Redfield, despite what you may think. Bears can be an important source for life-giving organs and nutrients, but these are long-term members of my collection. They are my most prized captives," he said.

"They look very healthy," I soothed.

"Every animal here is breeding," Kimura stated smugly, crossing his arms in front of his chest.

"Why would you want Tasmanian tigers to breed in Japan?" asked Isabelle.

"Mr. Kimura is a businessman," I answered for him.

"I would supply the world's zoos, taking the pressure off the native population," he said.

"Your animals would have to come from the wild. What if they didn't like it here?"

"They will like it here," said Kimura.

"But Tasmanian tigers are extinct," said Isabelle.

"Six million Dark dollars and a set of notes say otherwise," said Kimura.

"He wouldn't offer it if he thought there really were tigers," Isabelle flared.

"I could raise the stakes," Kimura said, looking at me steadily.

"So could I," I responded.

"And I could raise them again."

"As could I."

"You don't have my wealth," said Kimura.

"I have enough to make that tiger cost you a hell of a lot of money," I responded evenly.

"We will see," he answered, and disappeared.

Within moments, Ikura showed up to return us to the city.

# Chapter 16

LATE THAT DAY Ikura delivered us to the Intercontinental Hotel in Tokyo. When we were safely behind closed doors, Isabelle ordered me into the bath.

"Yesterday was enough bathing for a while," I said.

"Take the hint and take the bath," she ordered.

I lay back in the tub, closed my eyes, and practiced martial arts breathing. Manipulating my *chi* calmed me and allowed me to focus.

I lay there, thinking about Kimura and Tinker and Nozawa and Pennington. The picture on the box that held the puzzle pieces was blurred, and a lot of the pieces were missing. I thought maybe the gentle force of my breathing would make everything fit, but it didn't.

Isabelle came in wearing a red camisole, fishnet stockings, black garter belt and high heels. She put one foot up on the rim of the bathtub.

"Wow," I managed.

Without a word she took my hand and pulled. I

stood up, dripping hot water into the tub. She took my damp head in her hands, drew me to her, and kissed me. When we both came up for air, she reached for a bar of soap, lathered up and began to wash me from head to toe, stopping for a long time approximately midway.

Dry, the camisole did a poor job of hiding her breasts. Wet, it did no job at all. My dripping hands stained the fabric dark around the areas I favored as she moaned and pulled my body to hers. The water and the silk formed a thin electric field between us. We ended up sharing the tub.

"I like this better than *geishas,*" she murmured.

"So do I," I said.

"Right answer, buddy boy."


That night we took a taxi to a nightclub.

"Roppongi," Isabelle directed the driver.

"Akasaka better. Roppongi very low class," he said shaking his head.

But the driver was outmatched, and we went to Roppongi, stopping in front of a small and expensive-looking nightclub. The doorman turned several people away while I paid the taxi, but Isabelle's looks gained us instant admission.

The inside of the club was loud enough for earplugs. The crowd swayed to the primitive beat of pulsing rap music.

"Give me John Lee Hooker," I said.

"What?" she screamed.

"Give me a Bach Brandenburg," I said.

"Were you *born* old or did you just become that way in kindergarten?"

One wall of the club was alive with images from cameras aimed down at the throngs. These were wired into a myriad of television monitors, creating a video wall like the one we had seen in the Ginza. The images coalesced randomly into a coherent picture of the dance floor, and then disintegrated abruptly into a panel of unrelated screens. Smoke rose knee-high around expensively dressed patrons trying to outdo each other on the dance floor. There were scantily dressed Western brunettes and the occasional Scandinavian blonde, most often on the arm of dapper Japanese men with thin cigarettes hanging from their lips.

Isabelle gyrated happily before me while I performed loose and fluid renditions of predetermined kung fu *katas*, movements designed to simulate multiple attack-and-defend scenarios. The couples around me were too involved with each other to pay any attention to me, but my instinctive scan of the room revealed several shabbily dressed Oriental men sitting too stiffly at the bar, their drinks untouched before them. I wondered how they had gotten into the club.

"You're exhausting me," Isabelle cried, collapsing against my shoulder after an especially fast number.

"It's an old habit. I got it in kindergarten," I responded.

She put her arms around me, gave me a deep kiss, and retired to the ladies' room.

The bartender met my request for fifteen-year-old Ezra Brooks bourbon without expression, pouring me a neat glass and collecting *yen* amounting to about thirty dollars. I imbibed deeply, allowing the comforting aroma of the charcoal-filtered bourbon to waft around my nose. When Isabelle didn't show up after fifteen minutes, I went to look for her.

The floor was more crowded than ever, and it took

work to make my way around. The beat had changed from rap to rock and roll, and the dancers around me bent lower, jumped higher, and generally made it more difficult to find Isabelle.

And then I saw her. Or more precisely, I saw a hundred images of her, and they were all being dragged off the dance floor kicking and twisting, mouths open in a scream silent beneath the din.

My mind was already computing her location from the angle of the camera as I raced across the room, fingers and toes tingling with *chi* as they always do before a fight. I broke couples apart and interrupted erotic dance rituals as I ran, mindful only of the disappearing image of Isabelle's wild eyes.

I found her on the far side of the bar, near a black door with a brass peephole. She flailed weakly in the grasp of her captors, her lovely face a ghastly contrast of white flesh and red lipstick.

I threw myself on the man at her neck, targeting his ribs just below the armpit, numbing his brachial plexus and forcing him to release her. He hadn't seen me coming, and he turned, full of surprise, just in time to receive the heel of my palm under his chin. He went down with a grunt.

The second man was tougher. He maintained his grip on Isabelle's waist, using her as a support for a vicious back kick that caught me just above the hip bone and lifted me off my feet. I crashed into the bar, not far from what remained of my glass of bourbon. The tumbler jumped with the impact, several people moved out of the way, and a cocktail napkin floated down onto my chest. I shook myself, stood up, and went back at him.

He maintained his grasp on Isabelle's hair while he fumbled at the black door with a key, swinging it viciously at my eyes when I came too close. I arm-locked the swing with an *aikido* hold, trying to bring him to his knees. He released Isabelle but reversed my grip, twisting my wrist painfully.

I had never trained in traditional Japanese karate, but I could tell he had, and that helped. There are certain do's and don'ts with those guys, like moving in circles to confuse what is essentially a linear system, and like being careful as hell not to get nailed by their feet. Years of practice on the Wing Chun wooden dummy had taught me to kick at punch range, and allowed me to develop power in short kicks. I stole his breath and lifted him high with a foot to the solar plexus, then followed him to the wall and dealt a vicious, twisting elbow strike to his temple. He slumped down quietly as I caught sight of the last man dragging Isabelle away.

Some guys move constantly when they fight. Others stand stock still, moving on the inside, constantly circulating *chi,* ready as a car idling in neutral. The last guy let Isabelle go when I got close and then stood as still as I did. I kept my eyes loosely focused on his upper chest, knowing instinctively this one wasn't going to be so easy.

"Somebody help us!" Isabelle yelled, her voice hoarse from her injured throat.

The Japanese were too busy minding their own business to pay any attention.

"Somebody call the police!" Isabelle yelled again.

At that moment, perhaps sensing that Isabelle's fear had distracted me, he struck. He was young and tall and quick and strong, and his reach was greater than mine. The blow was a sophisticated spiraling fist that penetrated my initial pivoting block. It would have hit home near my heart had I not suddenly shifted strategy to employ what my martial arts mentor Sifu Amos liked to call the "energy blanket." Instead of tensing up, I allowed my torso and limbs to go limp, but dense as molten lava. His strike passed me low and to the side, and I yanked him off balance and pulled his face into my knee.

Without waiting to see more, I grabbed Isabelle by the arm and propelled her towards the front door.

"You're hurting me," she wailed, trying to release herself from my grip.

I let her go.

"Walk fast, then."

"That's the first time I've seen you like that, Nestor."

"Let's hope it was the last time."

"It was frightening."

"You're safe, aren't you?"

"Yes. Thank you. Was it Kimura?"

"I don't know."

"What kind of country is this? Three men dragging me away and nobody pays any attention!"

Suddenly a poker-faced Japanese man stepped out of nowhere and put a Glock semiautomatic pistol to my temple. His clone did the same to Isabelle, the plastic gun brushing the mussed wisps of her blonde hair.

The two men hid their guns professionally under the shelter of their sportcoats, and with no fanfare at all hustled us back into the club and out the same black door that had almost swallowed Isabelle a scant three minutes before.

# Chapter 17

A BLACK NISSAN sedan was waiting for us in the alley at the back of the club. There was a third man behind the wheel, tending the idling V-8. Our abductors pushed us into the back seat, and the driver sped off. I twisted around, trying desperately to think of how I could use one man against the other with the four of us crammed against the doors in the back of the car. My movement alarmed the men enough to make them pull their guns, and they pressed them against our temples again.

"Who are you and what do you want?" I demanded, my breathing fast and angry.

"We're American citizens," Isabelle glowered.

My world travels have taught me that nobody—least of all the Japanese—cares whether I'm an American citizen or not. I decided to keep this pearl of wisdom to myself, and instead tried to calm my breathing and figure a way free.

"They don't care if we see where we're going. That

means they're going to kill us," said Isabelle in a cracking whisper.

"Let's hope you're wrong."

"I'm scared."

I was, too, but I didn't want to tell her.

We drove out of the humming bustle of nighttime Tokyo, heading due north on the expressway. The driver stuck to the fast lane, his foot to the floor, his face ghastly white under the bright moon. The car smelled faintly of garlic and strongly of nervous sweat.

Two and a half hours later, we veered off the main highway, and suddenly we were driving along a well-lit main street bustling with shops and restaurants and clubs, many of them open even though the hour was late. Isabelle eyeballed the door, asking me silently if we should jump for it.

"Remember what we learned in Roppongi. Nobody cares," I said.

The street ran for about a mile, and then suddenly the world outside the sedan grew darker as shadows flickered in the moonlight. Isabelle leaned for a look under the trees, and the man next to her tensed, reaching for his gun. She ignored him and peered out the side window.

"A forest," she breathed.

It was no ordinary forest, but a tall, cold one, the trees forming a high canopy. There was a soft cover of snow, deadening the hissing of the tires on the ground. Icicles hung from the trees like the beards of old Japanese men. Under different circumstances, I might have marveled at the natural beauty of the place. As it was, it felt like driving through an enormous tomb.

"Where are you taking us?" I demanded futilely.

"He doesn't speak English," said Isabelle.

And then the nightscape changed again, this time revealing huge dark pagodas, temples, and shrines. The light was uneven, but bright enough to reveal a myriad of intricate carvings and paintings, a veritable panoply of over-ornate gilt. The driver stopped the car and we got out. The two men with guns motioned us to the head of a long snow-covered path that led to a cobbled street on which stood a gigantic two-story building, like the others we had seen, but even more lavish, more extreme. I tested the ground, judging whether I had the footing to risk an attack, gauging the distance between Isabelle and the nearest gun. My eyes were busy, constantly scanning the buildings around us, looking for a doorway to duck into, a dark corridor that would hide us. The men drew closer.

"Monkeys," Isabelle said, pointing to the side of the building.

I didn't get it until the men took the bait, glancing at a carving she'd indicated. I made my move, sweeping the legs out from under the man next to me, and he went down reaching for his gun. His head hit the snow-covered cobblestone street with a thunk, and his pistol-seeking fingers went limp.

The other man was grappling with Isabelle, who hung heavy on his shooting arm while he pushed her forehead away with the heel of his hand in an attempt to keep her teeth from his wristbone. I relieved her of the fight by chopping the side of his neck brutally hard, causing a spasm in the carotid artery. He went down with fluttering eyes.

"Now what?" Isabelle gasped, shivering in her disco dress.

Her question was answered by the sudden reappearance of the Nissan sedan. We tried to run, but the slippery stones caught Isabelle's heels and the driver was out, Glock pistol in hand, before we had gone ten steps. He gestured ahead, keeping a wary distance, ignoring his fallen comrades. The three of us followed a white path that led around the side of the building.

"Stop!" said the driver.

Keeping his eyes and his gun on us, he edged his back against an elaborately carved door. I heard a buzzing, then a whirring sound, and the snow at his feet was illuminated in cold blue as the door slid open. He put his hand on my shoulder and guided us in, me first, Isabelle's hand in mine. The door closed behind us and we dropped suddenly. We were in an elevator.

The doors opened onto a brightly lit room full of computer screens and bustling with tense Japanese men wearing guns and carrying pieces of paper. One man separated from the rest and approached us.

"Americans?" he asked.

"He's dangerous," the driver nodded at me. "Miyako and Kozuru are injured."

The driver muttered something in rapid-fire Japanese and the other man looked at me curiously.

"Where the hell are we?" Isabelle demanded.

"You are at Interpol headquarters in Nikko."

"I don't believe this," said Isabelle.

"I need to see your commanding officer right away," I said evenly.

"I am Captain Chitose," the man answered.

"Well, Captain, you've screwed up. This is Isabelle Redfield, and my name is Nestor Dark. I am a former American police officer."

Chitose's eyes went wide.

"You are certain they were with Kimura?" he asked the driver.

"I followed them myself."

"My friend Ms. Redfield is cold and very unhappy. I am very unhappy. Unless I get happy soon, I will make phone calls which will make *you* very unhappy," I said.

"Of course," he said hastily.

We followed him to an office separated from the main floor only by glass. The driver followed us, his gun still drawn, but now pointed slightly down.

"Get help for Kozuru and Miyako," Chitose ordered.

The driver holstered his weapon and turned reluctantly away.

I opened my palms. "I'm sorry about your men."

"So am I. Now please explain your presence at Mr. Kimura's home at Bandai," he began.

"Is there some law against that?"

"Please, Mr. Dark. I apologize for the rude way in which we brought you here, but this office is investigating Mr. Kimura and his business associates."

"So am I," I said.

"Not in Japan."

"Yes in Japan," said Isabelle.

Chitose gestured above his head, and a man came into the office.

"Perhaps you would take the lady outside while Mr. Dark and I talk," he said.

The man went for Isabelle's arm.

"I'm not going anywhere," she said.

"She stays or you get nothing," I said.

Chitose sat back in his desk chair and made a temple of his fingers.

"Bring Miss Redfield a blanket," he ordered.

When I was finished, I asked Chitose if I could count on Interpol's help.

"The question should be, can we count on yours?" he replied.

"I gather you brought us here because you thought we were doing business with Kimura and you wanted to squeeze us," I said.

Chitose remained silent.

"Why do you want him, anyway? Canned hunting? Smuggling?" I pursued.

"Police business, Mr. Dark."

"Seems to me like Nestor's hands and feet did your police business for you," Isabelle remarked, still fuming.

Chitose smiled. It was a good smile, replete with wrinkles and teeth, and it broke the tension in the room.

"Actually, you are lucky we took you when we did," he said. "There was a car full of Kimura's men on the street outside the club. They were armed."

"What would they want with us?" asked Isabelle.

"Even for a man like Kimura, five million dollars is a lot of money," Chitose replied.

"Is it smuggling?" I repeated.

Chitose nodded. "He has a way of coming up with animals there seems to be no way to get."

"His collection?"

"We can't prove it, but we're looking into it. We feel sure that he must have a contact, someone who is able to furnish him or his agents with the papers necessary to go after endangered species, and once they are either captured or killed, to export the living animals or their remains out of the country of origin.''

''Anything else?''

''Why don't you tell *me*, Mr. Dark?''

''All right. I think that Kimura has an interest in Tasmania that goes beyond the thylacine.''

''Such as?''

''I don't know. I'm not privy to his business connections, and my visit with him was perfunctory at best.''

''They did some shooting together,'' said Isabelle. Chitose smiled.

''Your reputation as a marksman precedes you. That must have been amusing.''

''Will you help us?''

''I went to Tasmania and I came to Japan for one reason and one reason only. I want to know who killed Joel Tinker. If your men come up with any connection between his death and Mr. Kimura, I need to know. In return, I will share any information I can uncover about Kimura's activities Down Under.''

''As I'm told you say in New York, you have yourself a deal, Mr. Dark.''

We shook hands.

# Chapter 18

ISABELLE WANTED TO get out of Japan as quickly as possible, and I didn't blame her.

"I always wanted to see the temples at Nikko, but I had a rather different tour in mind," she mused as an Interpol car drove us rapidly back to Tokyo through the spreading dawn.

"We're way off track here. We shouldn't have come."

"You needed to find Kimura."

I slammed my fist into my cupped hand.

"I needed to prove he killed Joel Tinker! I didn't do that. In fact, I didn't do anything at all."

"Now you know for certain he's behind the reward money."

"I knew that when his car met us at the airport."

"If we hadn't been at the airport, you couldn't have known."

I held my hand up.

"The only way to bring out the hunters is show them the game. I have to find a Tasmanian tiger."

\* \* \*

We collected our things from the Intercontinental and made straight for the airport at Narita. I called Arnet from the terminal and went through the usual charade with the desk. He called me back at the pay phone about five minutes later.

"A pay phone?" he asked.

"Narita. We're on the way back."

"You met with Kimura?

"Yes."

"Is he your man?"

"He's behind the money, if that's what you're asking."

"Will you stop back in Sydney? There's business for you here."

"There's business for me in Tasmania."

"You need to be here, Nestor. Kimura's involved."

"I'll be there," I said slowly.


Isabelle was making noises about the plane leaving without us, but I had to make one more call. This one was to Captain Giuseppe Rignola in New York. Some rookie patrolman was at his phone.

"The captain ain't here right now," he informed me.

"When is he expected back?"

"How the hell should I know? He doesn't have to answer to me, he's the captain."

"What's your name, officer?" I asked.

"Patrolman Kenneth Riley."

"I need to leave an important message for him, Riley. Can I count on you to give it to him?"

"And just who the hell are you?"

"A friend of his. I'm calling from Japan."

"Yeah? That how come you sound so far away?"

"That's how come."

"What did you say your name was?"

"Dark. Nestor Dark."

There was a pause over the line long enough to think that something had kinked the transoceanic line.

"I heard of you."

"I'm glad. Got a pencil?"

"Yeah. Go ahead."

"Tell him I need him to call U.S. Fish and Game, and find out whether an export license for Puerto Rican amazon parrots has been issued to anyone in Japan. Specifically, a guy called Kimura. You got that?"

"Parrots? You sure you got the right Captain Rignola?" Riley asked suspiciously.

"Just give him the message, will you Riley?"

I gave him the number to Macquarie House, and he grudgingly agreed to pass on my request to Rignola. Isabelle pinched my elbow and rushed me toward the gate.

"What was that all about?" she asked as we boarded the Boeing.

"Just a hunch," I said.

"You called Rignola on a hunch?"

I nodded.

"You know that's going to cost you, don't you?"

"I was paying cop debts before you were born," I said.

To an American, Australia is the more alien landscape, but—probably because of the attitude of the people—Japan is actually the less accessible. When the plane touched down in Sydney, Isabelle breathed a sigh of relief.

"It's got kangaroos instead of deer, but it feels like home," she said. "I'm glad to be back."

"So am I."

Arnet arranged to have us installed in the same suite we had left two days earlier. Isabelle napped while I went straight to Arnet's suite next door.

Three guests were sitting around a conference table bigger than the king-sized bed that Isabelle occupied one door away, and the room was thick with cigarette smoke. Arnet called me his trusted friend and business associate and introduced me first to Ian Mc-Cullough, a florid-faced, thickly-built Australian of Irish stock. I judged him to be in his late twenties, with a thirst for six or more beers a day. He told me he was a forest management specialist, and looked nervously at the man next to him for approval every time he wiped his nose.

That man was called John Bilkes, and he was alert and thin and hungry. His Adam's apple protruded like the prow of an old Cadillac. Bilkes told me that while he was the managing director of Australia's largest milling company, he was there as a representative of an industry consortium.

"John wants to keep the fate of Australia's timber in Australian hands," Arnet explained with a smile.

The last man rose languidly from the table and shook my hand warmly. He was tall and beanpole thin, like a Caucasian Waku.

"Rob Frank," he said.

"Rob is here representing the Green Independent Party," said Arnet.

Bilkes got up and walked to the chalk board at the end of the table. A huge map with plastic multicolored overlays obscured the writing surface. Rob Frank pushed a key across the table, identifying the areas on the map as regions that were owned by the government and up for logging contract, national parklands off limits to timber interests, and lands that were owned or leased on contract to a variety of milling outfits. Tasmania was part of the map, and my eyes went immediately to the region where Joel Tinker had believed thylacines endured. These areas were overlaid in blue, indicating that they were government owned, but available for logging.

"Australia's environmental protection laws prevent certain timber operations. That means, for example, that we cannot make paper using certain types of bleaches, which other countries allow. Those countries buy our timber, then sell the paper back to us. Costs a lot," Bilkes explained.

"Would Japan be one of those countries?" I ventured.

"I told you he was a quick study," Pichaud said, smiling.

"Japan has thus far been a customer of our wood chips, which they make into paper. They then compete with us on the world market," Bilkes continued.

"But there's threat of a Pacific free trade zone," said Pichaud.

"How would that hurt Australia?" I asked.

"The Japanese are achieving hegemony in this area a little bit at a time," Bilkes answered. "If they succeed in putting up an economic wall around the Pacific Rim, they'll become an even bigger fish than they are now."

"And they'll control your import, export, and pricing," I finished.

Pichaud folded his hands in his lap and smiled.

"Their environmental policies are nightmarish," I observed.

"Bravo," said Rob Frank.

"This meeting is about how to keep Australian wood and paper under Australian control," said Arnet.

"Is Tasmania involved?" I asked.

"Tasmania represents one of the greatest concentrations of timber in Australia," answered McCullough.

"The southwestern area as well?"

"It's a national park, but there's talk of shifting the boundaries around, allowing some logging," said Frank, gesturing at the map.

"Foreign interests are after the timber, then?" I asked.

"The Dutch," said McCullough.

"And the Japanese," Arnet added.

"Your proposition?" I asked Bilkes.

"Our proposition, Mr. Dark, is to make the Australian government an offer they can't refuse," he answered.

'I hope it includes plans for reforestation? If you keep cutting down the trees, anything that breathes oxygen will have more to worry about than paper and furniture," I said.

"We're proposing quick-growing trees," answered McCullough.

"And a promise for *clean* domestic milling," Frank added.

"Interested in putting some Dark money into the project, Nestor?" Pichaud asked brightly.

Three faces turned my way.

"Something can probably be arranged," I said, knowing full well that Arnet wouldn't be in on it unless there was a profit hiding somewhere in the deal.

# Chapter 19

ISABELLE WAS UP, dressed, and pacing furiously around the room when I returned.

"Thank God you're back," she said, as I shut the door behind me. "Waku has been calling the New York office every hour since last night. We didn't leave him any way to get hold of us, and apparently Arnet's office wouldn't give him our address. There's some kind of emergency in Strahan."

I picked up the phone instantly, and dialed Macquarie House. I could hear the relief in Graham Pullman's voice when I identified myself.

"What the hell's going on?"

"Your man Waku is right here, Mr. Dark. I think I'll let him explain."

Before I had time to inhale, Waku was on the line.

"Julie's gone," he said abruptly. "Disappeared the morning you left."

"What do you mean 'disappeared'?"

"She took off in her airplane. Just like that. Didn't say where she was going."

"Did she say when she would be back?"

"That's just it, Detective. She asked Divac to pack her a box lunch and told us she'd be back for dinner."

"Have you called the police?"

"After what you and I went through?"

"Okay. We'll be on the next flight. You just sit tight."

"What is it?" Isabelle asked as I hung up.

"Julie's gone," I said. "Disappeared in her seaplane."

Isabelle put her hand to her mouth.

"What do you think happened?"

"I have an idea, but let's wait and see."

I picked up the phone and called the Australian Aeronautics Board in Sydney. They connected me with air traffic control in Melbourne.

"I need to report a missing aircraft," I began.

The traffic officer was professional and to the point, and he listened carefully to the story.

"You don't actually know that it's missing. She could have changed her plans and landed at another field," he pointed out.

"Check her flight plan. I'll bet you'll find she went south into the Gordon-Franklin area and didn't report coming out."

He kept me on the phone for a few minutes and then came back.

"Are you sure of your dates, sir? There are several flights logged in the computer with that call sign and general flight area, but the last one is for the day *before* you claim Ms. Iringili departed."

"Yes, yes, she went up the previous day, too. I went with her. Nothing more recent?"

"I'm afraid not."

I hung up.

"She must not have wanted anyone to know where she was going," said Isabelle.

# Chapter 20

I GUNNED THE Fairlane up the driveway at Macquarie House, spitting gravel all the way to the parking lot. By the time I had the car in neutral, Waku was at my door.

"Any word?" I asked.

He shook his head. Isabelle got out of the car and took his hand.

"I'm sorry," she murmured.

"Nozawa's gone, too," he said.

"What?" I thundered.

"Pullman says he didn't pay his bill."

"I'll need your help," I told Waku.

Graham Pullman chose that moment to appear.

"I'll get us unpacked and speak to New York," said Isabelle. She went into the inn.

"Where have you put the shipping crates Ms. Redfield brought along?" I asked Pullman.

By way of answer, he led us around back to a shed he used to store gardening tools and a small lawn tractor. The three crates were in there.

''You running corpses?'' he asked with a faint smile.

Not me,'' I answered.

''I was going to suggest that you might want to call the air traffic controller in Devonport. I don't know about Ms. Iringili, but some of these bush pilots file some sort of plan when they take off.''

''It's done. She didn't file one,'' I answered.

Waku looked at me in surprise, but I was already busy opening the first crate. Pullman's curiosity was burning as brightly as the Tasmanian sun, and he would have stayed to watch if Waku hadn't shot him a foul look.

''You should be nicer to him; he's our host. None of this is his fault. He's a harmless man,'' I murmured as Pullman moved off.

''Why didn't she call Melbourne?''

''I don't know.''

''You think maybe she didn't want anyone to know where she was going?''

''Open the other two crates and lay the pieces out like I showed you last time. I'll be right back.''

He nodded, glad for a task that would take his mind off Julie.

I went upstairs to find Isabelle on the phone with the Dark Foundation answering service. She scratched messages for me on a pad, the phone tucked against her shoulder and obscured by a cascade of blonde hair. Soothed by her industry, I went to the closet for the locked case in which I had stored Joel Tinker's notes.

I flopped the case onto the bed, dimpling the down comforter, and dropped to my knees. Sunlight streamed over my shoulder, and I examined the face of the lock with a jeweler's loupe. There were small scratches on the surface.

The little green LED under the flap of fabric at the back of the case was illuminated, but I didn't need it to tell me that someone had been in the case. Joel Tinker's notes were gone.

Isabelle hung up the phone when she saw the look on my face.

"Nestor, what's the matter?" she asked.

"Joel Tinker's notes. The ones with the map. The ones that show where to find the tiger."

She stared at me.

"You don't think Julie . . . ?"

"I don't know."

"Did you copy the notes?"

"Of course. But that doesn't change the fact that someone else has them now, and that someone is a thief."

Downstairs, Waku had already finished laying out the pieces of my Ultrabat airplane.

"I knew I could count on you to find her," he said.

"You trust me at the stick?"

"Long as you don't run into any thunderstorms," he said, making reference to the tangle with an embedded storm over Denver that had nearly cost me my life.

I started my check of the fuselage. The composite parts had been beautifully assembled for me by the California company that usually sells just the kit, but I was worried about stress cracks from the flight over in the belly of a jet.

"You still think about Dolores, the schoolteacher who got caught in the crack war crossfire?" I asked.

"How do *you* know about Dolores?" he answered, real surprise on his face.

"You think you're the only informer in town?"

He nodded. "I hope you never get to feel that feeling. A woman dying on you, I mean."

I lifted the propeller onto the end of the Rotax 583's crankshaft while I thought about whether I should say what was on my mind. I secured the propeller and turned to face him.

"You're too late," I said.

He looked up from the ground.

"Before your uncle died?"

"While I was at the police academy."

"Somebody killed her?"

I shook my head.

"She was born dead, but she was stubborn. Her heart only had one chamber. Whacked out every time it had to pump hard. No workouts, no running for the bus, no life expectancy, but she managed a life."

"How come she lived to meet you?"

"She was careful and she didn't want to die."

"What was she called?"

"Rachel."

"Perhaps she disturbed one of the Ancestors."

"She didn't disturb anybody."

"Could be she went on a long journey."

"I'm sure she did."

"Could be she came back as someone else. A bird, maybe. Even Isabelle."

"She and Isabelle were alive at the same time, Waku. No reincarnation. Sorry."

"You loved her, didn't you?"

"Like Dolores."

"That Dolores was something. Make a man light

in the head, drive him crazy in bed. You ever tell Isabelle about Rachel?''

''No.''

''You think Julie's dead?''

I finished my tour of the fuselage and set about dragging the right wing into position for attachment. Waku scrambled to his feet and helped me, taking the tip as I fitted the hardware. My back was to him.

''I think maybe we don't know Julie as well as we should, but no, I don't think she's dead.''

''So you think she's hiding?''

''I don't know.''

''You know something you're not telling me?''

''Not for certain, no.''

He looked at me a while.

''How about your best guess?''

''Somebody stole Joel Tinker's letter from my locked suitcase.''

He paled, picked up a blade of grass, and put it in his mouth.

''How did Rachel die?'' he asked finally.

''She choked to death on canned corn. All alone in her apartment.''

''So it wasn't her heart at all.''

I shook my head. ''It was mine.''

The wind picked up just then, nearly toppling the partially assembled aircraft.

''Looks like a storm is rolling in,'' said Waku.

# Chapter 21

BROCHETTE OF LAMB was on the menu that night, and as Divac served it, thin brown gravy laced with small globules of animal fat slid off the silver serving tray. He managed to twist so that it ran under his sleeve instead of onto the table. I had sautéed soybeans and scalloped potatoes. Waku didn't eat.

"I understand you are going to fly into the ravine tomorrow," Pullman said. Divac reappeared with red wine. Isabelle accepted some. I asked for bourbon. Divac looked disgusted.

"I have reason to believe that Julie flew along the Franklin. Would you take Waku into the harbor to retrieve the submarine?"

"The model. Yes, of course."

Divac returned with a glass of neat Scotch.

"We don't have bourbon," he said.

I told him it would be fine, but I knew I wouldn't drink it.

"It assumes tigers like to swim or drink," I answered Pullman. "Is that your impression?"

"I wouldn't have an impression," Pullman replied.

"I would have thought five million dollars would make everyone an expert," said Isabelle.

Divac tripped over something in the carpet just then, and nearly crashed into the serving cart.

"Money isn't everything," said Pullman, looking annoyed.

Gusting winds woke us the next morning, but the sky was blue and clear. At breakfast, everyone including Waku expressed the opinion that I should wait for the wind to die down. I ignored them. I knew what my airplane could do.

At 350 pounds dry, the Ultrabat is only slightly less sensitive to wind shears and gusts than an albatross. Unlike that giant seabird, however, the "bat" is maneuverable and agile, built for aerobatic competition with the aeronautical version of a hair-trigger. She'll pull the six "G's," run better than 120 knots, and spin and stall all day long. To me she's like the Starship's sexy younger sister.

I put in some supplies and clipped the air charts to the instrument panel. Isabelle helped me push the little bird down to the roadway, while Waku loped gracefully off to secure the road. Divac and Pullman watched from the veranda.

I started the engine, and it caught quickly and easily, sounding harsh and staccato through the tuned aluminum exhaust. The instruments checked out, and I let go of the brakes and pushed the throttle forward.

The Ultrabat put me in the air in less than five hundred feet of pavement. I pulled up on the stick and pushed forward on the throttle, and Macquarie House, its serious owner, petulant chef, resident ghosts, and bereaved chauffeur grew as small as termites.

My best guess was that Julie Iringili had stolen the map from my suitcase and crashed while tiger hunting. I didn't want to believe it of her, but the Andrew Dark method of problem solving, in which I am thoroughly schooled, holds that the simplest answer to a problem is usually the correct one.

Using Isabelle's photocopy of Joel Tinker's map, I followed the same path that Julie would have followed to the upper Franklin River, flying as low as I dared and scanning the glorious patchwork of silver and green through the plastic bubble that covered my cockpit. I flew over the mouth of the Gordon, and beheld my remote control submarine bobbing on the surface, beaming a beacon I knew Waku would follow, carrying a tape I couldn't wait to see. The wilderness beneath me was so perfect and undisturbed that even the wind created by my little propeller on the tops of the trees seemed an intrusion. I dropped John Lee Hooker's *Mr. Lucky* album into my compact disc player and set the volume just high enough so that the rasp of Hooker's vocal cords drowned out my engine.

I concentrated on the line of the river, letting the stick follow its undulations as if I were playing a video game, but I saw neither smoke nor a break in the thick, green, rain forest canopy. I reached the junction of the Gordon and Franklin and turned due south, following the twisting course of the Gordon past Angel cliffs on my left and the little Sprent River and King Billy Range on my right. The river continued its twisting and turning course, here thundering white water, there a broad, seemingly calm expanse, the only giveaway a fast-moving branch or leaf.

I flew farther south until the course of the river shifted, turning slightly eastward, fed by the Olga and cutting a persistent path through the hard rock of the Nichols Range. At Denison Gorge the Gordon accepted the final flow of the Denison, a major waterway that started way up northeast in the Prince of Wales Mountains.

The Gordon continued eastward and so did I, passing through Abel Gorge all the way to the mouth of the Serpentine River. The map showed that the river ended at the confluence of Gordon and Peddar Lakes, the latter—to the horror of the Greens—changed forever by hydroelectric damming from a remote and exquisite lake to a giant featureless swimming pool. I knew the history, but I was not prepared for the monstrosity of the Strathgordon Dam.

It was high and wide and concrete and gray, and it imposed itself on the formerly lovely riverine vista like a giant tumor I once saw at a coroner's autopsy. I wanted to overfly it and see the lakes and pipes and structures in greater detail, but I had been aloft for most of the morning and, despite the cross-country auxiliary tanks, I was running low on fuel. I banked in a long, low sweep across the face of the dam, an insect before the world's largest sheet of flypaper, and headed back down the river.

Julie Iringili and her seaplane and Joel Tinker's map remained missing, perhaps forever.

# Chapter 22

THE FORTY-MILE-PER-HOUR LANDING speed of the Ultrabat made putting down on the tarmac outside Macquarie House a pleasure. I kept the engine alight until I had nosed the tiny plane up almost to the edge of the lawn at the inn. Isabelle peeked through the bedroom window the same way I had a few days earlier, and then she was gone, reappearing a moment later in the driveway.

Before she could frame a question, I shook my head and asked after Waku.

"He and Graham went to pick up your submarine. The beacon came in. I have lots of messages from New York."

We went upstairs and she gave them to me while I cleaned up.

"Kevin Dilley is having a pizza party and he wants you to come."

Kevin Dilley was the president and chairman of Moreman, Inc., a robotics company I had helped launch with Arnet Pichaud's money.

"What's the occasion?" I asked, pulling off my shirt and splashing tap water all over my face.

"The fact that a robot is making the pie. It's a new model he hopes to sell to the pizza chains," Isabelle answered with a smile.

"I hope this doesn't cost a lot of enthusiastic Italian dough twirlers their jobs," I said.

"Why do you have to be such a killjoy. Kevin's so happy!"

"He *should* be happy. That company of his has made him a multi-millionaire."

"Money isn't everything," Isabelle scoffed.

"Now where have I heard that before?"

"My friend Sheila Greenstock called again about manufacturing healthy food for school children," she said.

"You know how I feel about Sheila."

"What are you doing? You just dried off."

"I decided to take a shower, okay? Why the inquisition?"

"I know we've talked about business with friends, but I think Sheila's idea is right in line with what we're trying to do with the Foundation."

"We?"

She smiled, and I stepped into the shower. She cracked the curtain and watched me lather and rinse the sweat that came from sitting under the bright sun in the tiny cockpit.

"In a nutshell, Sheila believes that diet is the root of all evil, that our dietary habits begin when we're children, and that the route to peace and prosperity— not to mention the easiest cure for so-called learning disabilities—is to change the way children eat."

"Sounds like a tall order," I said, watching her

watch me and keeping the conversation alive just to test her resolve.

"The company will deliver the food to schools cheaper than they can make it themselves. She'll buy in bulk, all organic."

"Organic produce is expensive," I said.

"She knows that. She's worked out the numbers. She spent ten years as a bookkeeper."

"How much does she want?"

"Fifteen thousand to do the first run for a school downtown."

"You giving me your word that she's not a flake?"

"I resent that. I already told you she's my friend."

"Business with friends is bad business," I said.

"Sometimes I worry about you, Nestor," she said at last.

"I'm glad somebody does. I worry about me, too."

"I worry that all your money puts you out of touch, that it's a kind of protective blanket that makes even sharp things dull. I'm worried that you forget just how hard it is for most people to just get through the day."

"You think I'm spoiled?" I asked her, poking my head out from under the running water.

"Not as spoiled as a lot of people with a lot less money than you have."

"Know why? Because my money doesn't make it any easier for *me* to get through the day."

"That's where you're wrong, Nestor," Isabelle said, leaning against the sink and looking sad.

"No. That's where *you're* wrong. All the money does is change what I have to think about. It changes my sense of scale sometimes, gives me different problems to work out. I am *hurt* by homeless and starving people, a garbage can world, greed, racism, vanishing species, injustice—all of it. Uncle Andrew blessed me by giving me a way to help. I'm not ashamed I'm not poor and helpless. Having money may not be politically correct, but it's a way for me to help and I do. Sheila can have the money, because she's your friend *and* because I think her plan has merit. Now quit judging me.''

She stuck her head into the shower and kissed me lightly on the chest.

''That sounded like a justifying speech, but I guess I'm the cause and I'm sorry,'' she said.

''Apology accepted. Now what else you got?''

''Microfiber rain hats,'' said Isabelle.

I smiled a little.

''Really. I read the proposal myself when it came in. Microfiber is a high-tech polyester. It breathes, lasts, sheds water, can be made to look like leather or wool or anything you please.''

''We're not in the fashion business.''

''But it's a miracle fiber!'' she protested.

''If it's really a miracle fiber, then get some samples to a couple of garment manufacturers. Amos Larsen might know a name; his father was in the business. See if we can get cheap blankets made for emergency relief work, donate them to the Red Cross or the United Nations.''

She stared at me for a moment.

''How much?''

''Fifty thousand dollars to start if they're really cheaper and better than wool. And I want a proposal from this guy costing out thermal underwear made with the stuff.''

''Thermal underwear?''

''It's a niche market, and people at sporting goods stores will pay anything to stay warm.''

''How do you know all this?''

I shrugged and made a grab for her wrist.

"I'm all dressed for lunch," she protested, pulling back a wet sleeve and shaking her dampened hair.

"Too bad you're not wearing microfiber," I said, grabbing at her elbow this time and pulling her completely into the shower.

"There was one more call. Some guy wants to sell you immortality."

"Immortality, huh? Well maybe I can buy it with the five million I make from the Japanese when I find that tiger."

She pushed me away for a minute, cupping my chin in her hand and looking at me searchingly.

"You're not just doing this for the money, are you, Nestor? I mean you don't *need* five million dollars."

"It was a joke, okay?"

I turned my face to the spray and cut the temperature down, letting the cold water cool me off. For some reason, nobody seemed to believe that I was in Tasmania out of loyalty to Joel Tinker.

"Anyway, his company makes this exact mold of you out of plastic, then they inject inert gases so you don't decompose, and they keep you that way forever," she said.

"Loyalty is very important to me. More important than living forever. It's quality, not quantity. I care *how* I live more than how long. Friends matter. Joel Tinker was my friend. My money brought him here, and he died here. I mean to find out why and by whose hand."

River-soaked, Waku and Graham Pullman showed up just in time for lunch. Waku carried my submarine awkwardly under his arm.

"Did you find anything?" he asked me anxiously.

"Nothing. But it was only a first pass. Thanks for retrieving the sub."

Divac appeared on the veranda to announce lunch, and Graham Pullman set up the videocassette recorder so that we could watch the screen during the meal.

The tape was surprisingly clear. Every once in a while the picture would wobble as the submarine hit an eddy or cross current which caused the stabilizers to kick in. There were moments, too, when we got a view of nothing but the shiny black surface of the Gordon as the camera swiveled from one bank to the other, controlled by a timer and a computer, scanning for tigers.

We ate quietly, the only sounds being the clink of silverware on china and the steady whirring of the VCR.

Divac brought braised blue shark in *beurre blanc* for the others, brussels sprouts with raspberry sauce for me.

"Are you certain you get enough protein?" Pullman asked me.

"He gets plenty," Isabelle replied.

Our four sets of eyes watched the tape intently as the little reel spun on, revealing the details of the river from a foreign elevation.

"Everything looks so small," Waku breathed.

"I think the trees look enormous," said Isabelle.

I ignored the surface and the trees and concentrated my gaze on the waterline, watching, hoping for the barest hint of a marsupial paw or the tiniest glint of a tiger's eye. I was watching that thin interface between river and land so intently that my mind didn't register the outline of the Cessna's tail until the film was already depicting a new piece of river.

"Stop!" Waku cried.

"I saw it!" Isabelle called out.

Graham Pullman wore his usual look of puzzled resignation. I got up and rewound the tape.

To Divac's dismay, everyone crouched on the floor by the television for the replay.

"There! Freeze the frame!" I said.

Pullman pushed the button and the picture stopped, wavering for a moment and then growing still. Flotsam and jetsam, pressed by the current, adhered to the piece of riveted metal.

"It's the Cessna's tail section," I said quietly.

"Are you sure?" Waku whispered.

"I'm sorry," I answered.

# Chapter 23

LEAVING HIS SHARK to cool on his plate, Graham Pullman hurried down to the dock to ready the *Phantasm* for another trip down the river. Waku and I furiously repacked the duffel while Isabelle looked on.

"Contact Lieutenant Pennington in Hobart. Let him know we've found the plane," I told her, leaving the number.

"If you were going to call him, why did you wait?" she asked.

"Because all we had up until now was a missing girl. Now we have a crash."

"And maybe a body."

"And maybe two bodies," I said grimly.

Waku and I drove the Fairlane the two blocks to the pier because we were impatient and the duffel weighed more than a hound from hell. Pullman had the *Phantasm* about as shipshape as an old boat could get. The teak decks were uniformly wetted down with fresh water from the cleaning hose, and the brass gleamed. Wisps of unburned diesel fuel, the very stuff that was turning the whole planet into one enormous yellow cloud, escaped from the stern where the twin engines burbled at idle, the exhaust churning the water and choking even the fish.

We had been aboard before and we knew the drill, so our departure was silent and seamless. Waku unhooked the stern line; I did the honors at the bow. We both jumped on as Pullman gently engaged the throttle and sent *Phantasm* out once more across Macquarie Harbor.

The afternoon wind had picked up, and the sky was that particular shade of shimmering blue that Tasmania had already imprinted upon my brain. Pullman aimed the deep "V" of the hull forty-five degrees to the whitecaps, so there was little bounce and shake. Waku was inside the cabin, my giant Steiner marine binoculars in his hands, staring through the forward windows at precisely nothing. I sat down in a space between the anchor and the forward hatch, deliberately blocking his view. He looked at me through the window and lowered the binoculars, his fingers still tight around the rubber.

"You won't see anything for a while," I yelled over the wind and the spray. "The wreck's at least three hours up the river."

"I want to be the first to see it," he yelled back. Something in his expression made me get up and move aside.

Pullman had a chart of the river in front of him, and when I got bored with the scenery I went in to help him with his calculations. I could tell that he was basically guessing where the wreck lay. I had a better idea. I picked up a pencil, braced myself against the dark wood wheel housing and the brass instruments, and started to figure on the edges of his chart.

"The tape records and plays back at the same speed. We watched this many minutes of tape before we saw the tailpiece. That means the sub had been recording for that length of time, minus the daylight. Multiply that length of time by the speed of the river current, and that gives us a distance."

He nodded, watching me.

"I put the sub in here, by the cave," I pointed at a spot on his chart. He seemed surprised that I could read it so easily.

"So all we need to do is measure off that distance and we're in the ball park."

I nodded and moved away from his instrument cluster.

"A little crude, but probably more accurate than doing it your way, just by the look of the vegetation."

"Changes in the riverbank are pretty precise. I've been cruising this water for quite a few years."

I shrugged.

"Your choice. Just find the airplane."

I knew that the hours had to be eating at Waku's heart, so I went and tried to get his mind off the numbing sameness of one wave after another, off the maddening slowness with which the mouth of the river grew larger and larger in the afternoon light.

"She drowned down there, didn't she?" he asked, still staring through the binoculars at nothing in particular, but using them to protect his moist eyes from my gaze.

"It's possible, yes."

He nodded slowly.

"Did she hurt?"

"I can't know that. I don't know if she's even down there. She might have been thrown clear. She might have racked up against a tree. We won't know until we're there."

"I'm afraid of her pain."

"You're afraid of your pain, not hers," I said gently. "Whatever she suffered, it's over already. You can't be afraid of something in the past unless it's going to have an effect on the future."

"Her being gone, that has an effect on my future," he answered, turning the binoculars so that their wide, blue-tinted ends were aimed at my face. If I ducked a little and turned my head to the side I could just make out his tiny yellow eyeballs, pinpricks of light at the end of what looked like a long glass tunnel.

"You didn't know her that long," I said.

"Still," he answered.

"Let's hope for the best, then. Let's hope she got lucky."

"She wasn't a good swimmer. She told me that."

I gave his thin shoulder a squeeze and left him to his pain and his doubt.

"Let's hope anyway."

As it turned out, neither Pullman's calculations nor mine needed to be very precise, because once we knew it was there, the tailpiece stood out as clearly as a compound fracture. Waku was, by his own design, the first to see it, so by the time it was abeam Pullman had already throttled way back. Even so, his screws wreaked havoc with the river, making the reflective black surface even more impenetrable.

"That river isn't giving anything up," I said.

"Who's going down?" asked Pullman.

"Waku doesn't swim any better than he says Julie

Iringili did,'' I answered, making for the stern stowage compartment where we had secured my bag.

''The detective, he does everything,'' Waku smiled wanly.

I think I know what it took for him to force his lips that way, and it was a brave smile.

The binoculars swung about his neck like a dead bird, like the weight of his fear, popping off his flesh in little rhythmic bounces with the beating of his heart.

I laid diving gear out on the deck.

# Chapter 24

AFTER THE STREET morphine I had gotten him for his pain pushed his respiratory rate lower than a deep sea clam's, Andrew Dark had taken my hand, instructed me to do something good with his money, looked me in the eye, and died. It took me time to close down his life, time to appreciate the deft and supportive way he had raised me, time to mourn him, and time to learn enough of the world to fulfill his dying wish.

For two years after his death, I educated myself on the road, and that road ran fast and far and had branches and detours I had never expected. One of those detours took me to the Berry Islands, a small archipelago off the Bahamas. I was there on a fishing boat owned by three boys from Miami who thought they could make it big in the charter business but had too much money and not enough hunger to stick to the original plan. I made their acquaintance in a bar in Nassau, and they had talked me into a few days of cruising and scuba diving. I assured them that my mother had taught me to swim in a YMCA pool, but

I admitted that everything I knew about diving I had learned from watching Jacques Cousteau on TV.

They were creatures of wealth and sloth, not at all the type of man I was trying to make of myself. But they made me laugh at my own seriousness, and I liked them. Out on the ocean with them, I practiced one-legged White Crane kung fu positions on the sea deck and was thrown overboard by a wave. They stopped the boat for me, but that was all they did. They didn't throw a life ring, they didn't let out a dinghy, they didn't even put down their margaritas.

But they did teach me to dive. If living on the edge of a vast tract of tropical ocean gave them anything, it was a love and respect for the ocean and a gift for understanding its marvels. They had first class equipment on board, and they knew how to use it.

I remember the way my pulse raced the first time the clear warm water closed over my head, and I remember the way I sucked on the regulator in my mouth as if I were trying to take it right down my throat, "O" rings and diaphragms and all. I used an hour's worth of air in fifteen minutes, struggling with the buoyancy compensator vest that had seemed so simple and straightforward on the surface, but now seemed impossibly sensitive to the change in density that each breath caused in my body.

So they hauled me out, and we went through the drill again. One of them, a kid who had taken three karate classes in high school, told me to think about the breathing lessons I had learned from the martial arts, to use what I knew to control my internal environment underwater just the way I did on land.

Those were the magic words, and once my breathing was under control, everything else came easily. The rhythmic whooshing sound of the air going in and out of my lungs was as seductive as familiar perfume. It wasn't the miracle of fishes or the beauty of coral reefs that beguiled me nearly as much as it was the silence. Within days, I was using diving as a shortcut to a meditative state that had taken me years to master in the *dojo,* and was using half as much air as the most experienced and slightest of my three friends.

And for all the poking and good-natured ridicule, they were gentle and patient teachers. They taught me what to do when my air ran out and habits to develop so that didn't happen. They taught me how to get into a cave by taking everything off underwater, slipping through a narrow opening, and then putting it all back on again while holding out a strong underwater light to make sure that nothing carnivorous had gone in there first. They taught me how to navigate in water so murky I couldn't see my own watch, and how to use a current instead of fighting against it. A week on the boat with them made me a competent open-ocean scuba diver, and I was sorry when the little boat put in again in Nassau—but not too sorry to help them put away a year's worth of tequila in one night.

Scuba diving became my favorite sport, and it remained that way until I learned to fly an airplane. My travels took on a diving theme, half because I enjoyed the high of the depths and half because I needed a theme to feel like I was accomplishing something. I dove the World War II wreckage in Truk Lagoon, the white coral walls of Fiji, the incredible reefs of the Red Sea and the vast kelp forests of the Scandinavian fjords. I even looked for Atlantis in the deep, round boulders of the Mediterranean. During the course of my travels, I learned the sport's technical side, and gained official certification in ice diving, cave diving, deep diving, and underwater navigation.

I had several encounters with sharks as big as my Aston Martin, and I watched a man drown in the Pacific off Santa Barbara, but none of it ever turned me off the silent undersea world for more than a few weeks. I felt peacefully alone there, and yet connected to the planet in a way maybe a non-diver can never understand.

And I learned to rely on myself.

# Chapter 25

PULLMAN AND WAKU stood by while I laid my equipment out on the still stern of *Phantasm*. I checked the "O" rings in my gear and visually inspected the hoses that linked my gauges and my mouth to the air in the aluminum tank. Satisfied, I fitted everything together in the latest aquadynamic backpack available. I preferred the Swedish "Poseidon" regulator, a finicky and expensive machine that required more maintenance than other units, but gave unparalleled breathing comfort and performance in cold deep water because of a thin cylinder of oil around critical moving parts.

I stripped to my shorts and pulled on my diving suit.

"What sort of wet suit is that?" Pullman asked, watching me intently.

"It's not. Wet suits use a layer of water close to the skin for insulation. That doesn't work so well in very cold water, because it takes a while for the body to heat it up, and the layer is constantly being replaced at the neck, wrists, and ankles. This suit is totally dry. The rubber at the elbows, wrists, and neck is watertight. So is this zipper I use to get in. I'll stay warmer this way.''

I put the suit on and immediately started to sweat in the summer heat of the late Tasmanian afternoon. I shrugged on the backpack one strap at a time and walked to the gunwale.

Waku steadied me while I donned my fins and inserted the mouthpiece, tasting the bitter rubber. I nodded when I was ready, raised my feet to the sky, and somersaulted backwards into the black river.

I knew the Cessna lay less than fifteen feet in front of me, but I couldn't see it at all. I switched on my underwater light, but it accomplished no more than high beams in a winter fog. I oriented myself against *Phantasm*'s dark hull, and swam aft, trailing my hands along her wooden planks. I sliced my fingertip on a barnacle and felt the sudden pain, but had to bring my finger almost to my face to see the tiny trail of blood move away from my face stupendously fast. I hadn't bargained for the strength of the current, and I was tiring too quickly. I rose to the surface. The sun was as brilliant as a dentist's lamp when I popped up. Waku looked worried and far away and small.

''Throw a line! The current's too strong!'' I yelled.

A thick yellow snake came spiraling toward me moments later, and I used it to pull myself forward to the anchor line. I changed lines then, pulling myself down towards the embedded anchor, holding my flashlight between my legs and aiming it ahead and down by swiveling my hips. The current pressed the mask hard against my face. My nose began to bleed. I let go of the line with one hand while I pulled the lower seal of my mask away to let the river wash in and clear away the blood and mucus. I nearly lost the mask then, and it was a struggle to regain the line.

And then, suddenly, Julie Iringili's floatplane was before me. I saw the strut first, the diagonal piece of metal that braced the wings for the extra weight of the pontoons and the shock of landing on water. It looked as white and wounded as a dead hooked fish. I could just make out the leading edge of the wing above it, but the floats were obscured by the fast-moving river. To get to the cockpit I was going to have to let go of the anchor line and close the five feet with a furious burst of swimming.

I steadied myself on the line for a few moments, breathing deep and easy. The current pressed my dry suit against my upstream side as if I were standing in a stiff wind. The downstream material billowed like a diva's skirt. I let go with one hand to transfer my lamp from my legs to my hand, angled myself into the current like a skydiver, and wrenched myself forward toward the sunken plane.

At first the Cessna receded, but I kicked and scooped water for all I was worth and she reappeared. I kicked until my fins vibrated with the conflicting forces and I finally got hold of the wing. I hooked my fingers into the space between the trailing edge and the flaps. Slowly, ever so slowly, I pulled myself toward the fuselage, my flashlight flailing on its tether around my wrist, affording me glimpses of a burned and twisted engine cowling and a propeller with only one blade.

I kicked and pulled myself back towards the passenger door, took a deep breath, hooked my arm around the wing strut, and shone my light inside.

\* \* \*

The cockpit was an empty shambles. The yoke was bent, most gauges broken, the whole instrument nacelle pulled from the front of the plane at an angle grotesque to any pilot. A microphone and two pairs of headsets floated lazily in the current, straining at their plugs. I played the light around the cockpit some more.

There were two sets of seat belts loose and floating, and the passenger seat had been moved forward on its rails. The door was downstream from the current and opened readily. I opened it because I had to.

I opened it because I saw Joel Tinker's map.

# Chapter 26

WHEN I SURFACED, Waku was leaning over the gunwale so far a feather landing on his head would have knocked him in.

"I followed your bubbles," he explained, his face twisted with the great anxiety of expecting the worst.

"She's not down there. Nobody is."

The look of relief on his face was indescribable.

"What did you find?" asked Pullman, taking my backpack from me and heaving it onto the deck.

"There were two passengers."

"How do you know?"

"The seats were pushed back, the lap belts unbuckled. Both doors unlatched."

"Couldn't that have happened during the crash?"

"Maybe the doors. Maybe the belts. Possibly even the seats. Not all three. It makes more sense that there were two passengers."

"The simplest explanation is always the best," Waku murmured, recovering enough to extend his hand and help me flop over the stern.

"I'm afraid I also found this," I said, reaching into the pocket of my dry suit and pulling out the drenched and tattered paper.

"A map?" Pullman queried.

"It's Professor Tinker's last letter to me. It held the location of the tiger."

"Julie stole it," Waku said dully.

"Julie, or whoever she was with," I answered.

"Either way, she was following it," said Pullman.

The letter had been hand-written in fountain pen on lined paper torn from the kind of composition notebook a third grader might carry, the type with the thin red line an inch or so from the left to help set limits for the would-be essayist. Barely a word of the original text remained legible.

Pullman extended his hand, and I gave it to him.

"The secret to the tiger," he said. A drop of water fell onto the deck, ending as a light blue stain on the teak.

"If there really is a tiger," I answered.

"And Julie?" Waku asked.

"The engine cowling is burned. The prop is half gone. My guess is she lost power at low altitude and went into the river with only flaps."

"What could cause such a thing to happen?" asked Pullman.

I shrugged. "A few possibilities. Maybe an ignition wire went bad, or a fuel line became detached and ignited on the hot block. We'll know after the experts have gone over it."

"Julie couldn't swim," Waku whispered, staring at his feet.

"She might not have had to. The tail is almost at the shoreline," Pullman offered.

"She might have gotten out," I said.

"Either way she's a thief." Pullman straightened, brushing his thick hair back with his hand.

"She stole nothing. It was the Japanese," Waku flared.

"You don't know that," said Pullman.

"Neither do you," Waku snapped.

"I'm sorry about Julie, but nobody really knows what happened here. You're right that we've all been thinking that Nozawa may somehow be involved, but until we find her we can't know," I said.

"You think she's still alive?"

"I'm more convinced of it than I was before I went diving."

"Do you know something about Mr. Nozawa that I don't?" asked Pullman.

I motioned them into the cabin, where I stripped off my dry suit and toweled off my sweat.

"He works, or worked, for a Japanese businessman named Kimura. It was Kimura who put up the reward. Ms. Redfield and I saw Kimura in Japan. He denied any knowledge of Dr. Tinker's death."

"Excuse me, but what are we going to do to find them?" Waku interrupted.

"Cruise the river one more time," I suggested.

"It's a shot in the dark. We don't even know which way they went," said Pullman.

"Back towards the harbor," said Waku.

Pullman shrugged.

"I don't think so. I think they're still on the hunt. Otherwise we would have seen a signal fire, a white flag, something along the river," I said.

"A message in a bottle?" Pullman smiled.

Nobody laughed.

# Chapter 27

PULLMAN PILOTED THE boat upriver while Waku and I scanned the bank from opposite sides of the bow. There wasn't much light left, and when the tree trunks grew as black as the river, Pullman dropped anchor and killed the engines. The lapping of the water mixed rhythmically with the cyclical humming of the boat's generators, and we swung back and forth until the bow stabilized against the current.

"I sure miss Divac tonight," I said wistfully.

"I'll drink to that," said Pullman, bringing forth a bottle of Wild Turkey from the cabinet beneath the ship-to-shore radio.

"Bet he doesn't miss *you*," said Waku, reaching for the bottle before I even had time to pour myself a taste.

I was astonished. In the years I had known Waku, I had never seen him evidence any interest whatsoever in alcohol or drugs. I had chosen him as an informant because he was so straight, figuring that, with a nose that clean, if he was still alive and connected on the street he must really have something on the ball.

"What the hell are you doing?" I asked.

"Chasing away the cold," he answered, tossing back half the glass.

Pullman watched, puzzled.

"He doesn't normally drink," I explained.

"Nothing's normal anymore," he slurred, obviously and instantly wasted. "Julie's out there where the tigers can get her, if they haven't already, with that Jap, all alone, at night."

"I'm sure Ms. Iringili can take care of herself," Pullman said, pouring himself two generous fingers.

Strong foreign smells drifted in through the open cabin door as the last glow on the horizon disappeared. Waku shivered.

"You didn't see blood or anything down there, did you, Detective?" he asked me.

"The only blood I saw was mine."

Divac had packed box dinners for us: *prosciutto* and dried figs for Pullman and Waku, cucumber on a wheat roll for me. Waku picked at the figs, teasing out each seed just to irritate Pullman.

"Wonder what would happen if you threw one of these overboard," he mused, inspecting the tiny pale seed on his fingertip.

"Some fish would eat it," Pullman responded tightly.

"Fish food. That's about all this shit is good for," Waku said in disgust.

Pullman asked me how I knew Joel Tinker, and I told him we were childhood friends.

"Close enough so that he would call *you* from Zeehan."

"My foundation gave him the grant for his research."

"But you told me you didn't know of the reward."

"He didn't do it for the money," Waku interjected. "He was helping out a friend."

"And I believed in the project," I said.

"You were curious?"

"About the existence of the tiger? My foundation is committed to conservation issues, and I knew Joel Tinker's goal was to find and protect the last of the species."

"You don't think he was in it for the reward?"

"Joel was one of the smartest men I've ever met. If money had been important to him, he could have done almost anything with his life. As it was, his calling chose him. He believed that other living creatures have a moral right to occupy the planet right along with us—and I agree with him."

"I'm not much on animal rights. I bet the five million had more to do with his Tasmanian venture than you know." Pullman smiled cynically and took a sip of bourbon.

Waku wandered off to lie on the foredeck under the stars. Pullman offered a game of backgammon.

"Backgammon's not too big in America anymore. I used to play with my uncle, years ago," I said.

"Be surprised how many of my guests play," he said, carefully setting up the pieces.

We rolled and he won the first move. It was "lover's leap," a classic combination that enables men trapped behind enemy lines to leap cleanly to safety. My own roll was much more pedestrian.

I learned a lot about Graham Pullman at the backgammon board. He refused to play unless we put a few dollars on the game, and his strategy showed a risk-taking streak I would never have attributed to him. The dice were with him, and he won the first game handily.

"It's a dice game. A tyro can beat a master almost anytime if the rolls don't turn out right."

"You're too modest," I replied, forking over the five bucks I owed him.

He won the second game too, and with it another fiver, but once I understood that he was bound to risk by the thrill of it, I was able to capitalize on his rashness. I played a back game, leaving my men in his home board far longer than I might with a different opponent, assuring myself of plenty of ammunition as he recklessly left men unprotected in a mad rush to overwhelm me. I used the doubling cube to raise the stakes to ten dollars and won three more games from him, driving the bourbon bottle deeper and deeper down his gullet. He wanted another round, but I swore off and bunked down in the forward cabin where the two mattresses came together in a V at the hull.

Several hours later I was awakened from a whiskey-drenched sleep by a series of small scrapings and a sudden flash of light. I peered cautiously through the slats on the door that divided my cabin from the common area.

Pullman, still dressed from the day's sail, was bent over the chart table. I glanced at Joel Tinker's watch. It was 3:00 A.M. I pushed on the white ceramic knob and felt the metal restraining clips let go of the doors. I crept forward until I could see that what lay on the table was the still damp and tattered copy of Joel Tinker's map.

Pullman traced the diffused blue lines with his fingers, referring back and forth between Tinker's map and his navigational guide to the river. His lips moved soundlessly, revealing the intensity of his concentration. Years of martial arts training had taught me to contract my *chi* into a tiny dense ball in my *tan-tien*, an area below the navel and above the pubis. This contraction had the effect of withdrawing my presence from the physical space around me. Thus drawn in, I was hard to notice. It was a technique that had served me while on the street as a cop, and most especially during SWAT team surveillance.

And it worked in the little teakwood cabin with Graham Pullman. I stood for several minutes while he grunted and clucked quietly over private information he had no right to whatsoever. When I was satisfied with his intent, I lunged forward in a martial blur and snatched what remained of the letter from his grasp. He jumped back.

"What the hell do you think you're doing?" I demanded. The boat vibrated with my voice. Waku stirred up front under the moonlight.

"I was just trying to figure out where we should go tomorrow. Which way they may be traveling."

"Assuming they're still on the tiger hunt and not just trying to get away."

"They must still be on the tiger hunt. It's why we're all here."

"It's not why *I'm* here."

"When you hunt you have to think like the quarry."

"This isn't a hunt, it's a rescue mission," I said.

"Maybe hungry tigers like the smell of human blood," said Waku from the forward hatch.

''Maybe hungry tigers are wishful thinking,'' said Graham Pullman, switching off the light over the chart table.

I went back to bed thinking hard about who was wishing for what. I had a hell of a time falling asleep.

# Chapter 28

A BRIGHT MORNING sun washed *Phantasm* in brilliant, glimmering Tasmanian light. The three of us rose like zombies from the grave, simultaneously called forth by the glow. We stumbled around the cabin, splashing cold water on ourselves, letting the bourbon out through our breath and our spit and our sweat.

"Which way this morning?" I said at last.

"Back toward the harbor," pronounced Graham.

"The detective flew over all that," Waku protested.

"He flew over the plane wreck, too. We're basing everything on the assumption that they've stayed close to the riverbank. Maybe they're way inland. Running the river could be a waste of time," said Pullman.

"The bush gets too thick away from the river. They just can't be far from the water," I said.

"The bush is thick everywhere," Pullman muttered.

While we drank instant Nescafe, I doodled some figures on a piece of paper.

"Let's assume they're hurt. Not too hurt to walk, but hurt enough to go slower than healthy hikers might."

"Let's assume they're hungry," said Waku.

"They're hungry; they may be injured; Nozawa may be forcing Julie along."

"I don't buy that it's Nozawa. But if it is, why does he want her along?" asked Pullman.

"Maybe she knows the bush better than he does. Maybe he doesn't want to kill her. Maybe he can't let her go for fear she'll get back to civilization and get the police after him."

"No way they'd believe her," Pullman muttered.

"And why might that be?" asked Waku, rising from the table.

"You both embarrass me. We're out here to save victims of an air crash, not squabble like a couple of *prima donnas*. Now I'd say that making two miles per hour and walking nine hours a day, they'd have made 27 miles by now. That's a couple of more hours for us. I say we go upriver."

Waku retired again to his favorite spot on the foredeck while Pullman raised the anchor, and we made for Tigerland.

Pullman spotted an area of light growth along the bank and dropped anchor. Waku and I shouldered a couple of day packs and jumped ashore.

Despite the fact that he was raised in mainland Australia's arid interior and hadn't tracked anything more than a violent john in twenty years, Waku read secrets in the vegetation it would have taken me years to divine. I watched his nose flare, his fingers twitch, and his body accordion to the scents of the river shrubs as we made our way through the dense foliage, stepping over the thick, complex root systems of the Huon pine and sassafras and myrtle. None of my martial arts training, none of my quiet rooftop time behind a sniper's rifle, prepared me for trying to stay with Waku in the bush. I felt like an elephant following a ghost through a spider web.

At last he stopped, and I came up behind him, my back wet with sweat, concentrating on breathing through my belly as Sifu Amos Larsen of Greenwich Village had taught me to do, trying to stabilize my body and get control of the rush of my senses. Graham Pullman's boat was already a brown speck down the twist of the river.

"Something big has been through here," Waku murmured, rubbing a myrtle leaf through his long fingers.

"Julie?"

He shook his head.

"Someone else?"

"If I were up north I'd say a large dingo."

"But there are no dingos here." I held his eye.

"No."

"Are you telling me you're tracking a tiger?"

"Ancestral knowledge doesn't flow that way. There's nothing in my past, nothing that my father or my mother, my uncles or my brothers have given me that would allow me to know that."

"You're saying you've never seen a tiger, so you wouldn't recognize his spoor."

"I've seen them in the dreamtime, but we're not sleeping now." Waku smiled sadly.

Back aboard the boat, Waku and I resumed our positions and continued to scan the riverbank while

Pullman piloted lazily down the Gordon. My eyes grew tired of staring at acre after acre of dense green foliage, and I started to imagine things, shadows among the trees, shapes put together by the tendency of my visual cortex to make organized information out of random green lines and dots. I took the glasses from my eyes, blinked, resumed the scan. But there was nothing but crisp, shimmering air, wet and earthy smells, and the paradoxical combination of a superficially monotonous but highly detailed and changeable naturescape.

By the end of the afternoon, the burn extended from the surface of my eyeballs to the back of my head. Pullman threw the anchor out, and the hull was once more at the mercy of the inexhaustible river. Waku immediately went to sleep in the fading sun on the foredeck. Pullman offered backgammon and bourbon, but I declined and went to bed.

# Chapter 29

I AWOKE LATER because it was cold. I lay in the bunk for a time, then dressed, got hold of my pocketscope, and went quietly ashore.

There was less than a quarter moon. I held the scope up to my eye, scanned the augmented landscape, and moved as quietly as I could through the trees. The river was profoundly different in the dark, a living presence swelling and contracting beside me like a giant sleeping beast. The scope revealed great detail, but a flash of intuition made me put it away. I sat down against a tree and practiced *Shing-Yi* breathing until my eyes cleared, letting the air fill my lower stomach like a pitcher and then exhaling as if I were pouring water off the top.

*Shing-Yi* is an esoteric internal Chinese martial arts system. Daily Hsing-I practice over time changes the body profoundly, making brittle tendons and bones supple as thick rubber and developing the level of the bioelectric life force the Chinese call *chi*. Although my training in Wing Chun boxing still dominated my moves, I was becoming more and more interested in the benefits of the internal arts, and Amos Larsen was obliging me with deep and fascinating instruction into what is perhaps the deadliest of all the fighting forms.

Standing among the fragrant branches, with the river running beside me, I felt hyperaware, astonishingly whole, and powerful, one with the fabric of things, and capable of striding across the land without the nightscope.

So I did. At first fear of tripping over a root or rut made my steps falter, but gradually I found that I could pierce the landscape the way Waku did when I'd followed him. My training came from a different continent, but it must have been made of the same stuff, because soon I was gliding through the thick underbrush like an Olympic figure skater.

The vegetation changed as I moved away from the riverbank. The trees—to my unaided eyes a dark canopy of wavering umbrellas—grew taller away from the water, and the space beneath them, instead of being crowded by roots, opened up into a field of low-growing ferns. I could walk between these without difficulty, rarely breaking a frond. Nesting birds ruffled their feathers as I passed below, and I heard tiny, unidentified creatures scurry through the underbrush ahead of me in frenetic bursts. The forest beguiled me.

Perhaps half an hour in from the safety of Pullman's boat, I became aware that I was being watched. Distracted, I tripped, and when I struggled to get up, found my boots caught beneath some vines. I tried to break them off, but they were too thick to break easily, and I had to squint in the night to find their source and pry them loose.

I noticed the smell before I heard anything, a rancid smell like bad milk poured over rotten apples. Joel Tinker had described it; Julie Iringili had referred to it. I yanked hard at the vines and jumped to my feet, and when I did, the tiger crashed away through the underbrush.

It *had* to be a tiger, and I wanted a glimpse of those stripes. I ran harder, faster, into the night, the pistol and scope in my knapsack hammering against the middle of my back with every bounce, the animal sounds fading against the scratching of my own clumsy footwork.

I stopped and listened, but the sounds were too far away for me to be sure of the direction. I ran a little further anyway, hoping I would wind whatever it was, knowing I wouldn't.

And suddenly the sky was gone.

# Chapter 30

IT WAS SO dark that I couldn't see my belt buckle, and I had to hold my fingers close to my face to be sure they were even there. I tried some deep breathing as the faraway sounds I had been following dwindled and disappeared. The air passing in and out of my lungs sounded like a typhoon. I shrugged my knapsack over my shoulder and took out the pocketscope.

I was standing beneath what appeared to be a dense carpet slung between the trees. For a moment, I was afraid that I was about to fall victim to a long-forgotten drop net installed by a tiger hunter long dead, but when I adjusted the pocketscope it revealed details: twigs and branches and leaves, all growing the wrong way. I remembered Julie's explanation of horizontal growth.

And then I heard sounds again, more muffled than before, like soft flesh instead of hard muscle, whimpering, as if the tiger had made a kill.

The pocketscope served up the night in vivid detail. I was close to the river again. I walked as quietly as I could this time, keeping my eyes down to avoid grabbing roots.

I nearly missed the opening to the cave. It was a slender, vertical crack in the riverside rock, and it showed as a black slit in the viewfinder. I paused outside it and heard the soft sound again. I leaned closer. I stepped on a twig.

Nozawa grabbed me before I could reach for the Wildey. The view through the scope was interrupted by what turned out to be his hand, and for a moment I was blinded by my own dependence on failed technology. He knocked the scope from my grasp and landed a solid rear punch to my gut. It winded me and I fell back. Then there was another blow, this one to the temple, and then an abrupt combination designed to weaken me enough so he could take my pack. My mind was dazzled by the darkness, confused by the onslaught, distracted by the whimpers of what had to be an injured Julie Iringili in the cave.

But Nozawa was predictable. Like Japanese tournament fighters I had met in the ring in my teens, his motions were linear, not circular. I dropped to my knees to step out of his range and drove a vertical fist into his groin. He doubled over, breathing hard, then stood and tried to kick my head. I rolled on my shoulder and came up ready. He came in again, this time with vicious front punches, uppercuts, and backfists. I used circling blocks to move his body first one way and then the other, punishing his ribs with *Shing-Yi bong* strikes, knuckle punches with great penetrating power.

"Waku?" I heard Julie's voice.

"Nestor," I managed, lifting my leg and delivering a devastating close range kick to Nozawa's cheek.

I saw him pirouette and was sure he was going down, but instead he took off into the underbrush.

"Are you all right?" I called into the cave, never taking my eyes from Nozawa's retreating back.

"My arm is broken."

"I'll be back. Just stay where you are."

I retrieved the pocketscope from the ground and sprinted off after Nozawa.

I felt a surge of panic when for a moment I thought I had lost him, but the pocketscope revealed his wiry frame halfway up a tree.

I grabbed at the trunk and began to climb. It was a giant eucalyptus, and the branches were widely spaced. I shimmied up, my body pressed against the rough bark. He was a faster climber, but my reach was longer and I was gaining on him. I tried for his foot, but he kicked at me viciously. His boots had rubber soles but steel toes.

And then he was gone again. The legs I had been following simply disappeared. At first I thought he had worked his way around to the other side of the tree the way a frightened squirrel might, but then I realized that he had simply stepped off.

The horizontal growth attached itself to the gum tree in a unique fashion, with branches that grew toward the trunk instead of away from it. Nozawa was crawling across the growth on all fours. I paused at the flimsy junction of leaf and wood.

I have never been much for heights. In my first year with NYPD, I had wavered at a window and cost a partner his life. He had exacted my promise to get over the problem before he died, and I had. I flew airplanes.

But I didn't walk across twigs thirty feet in the air. Nozawa got carefully to his feet and began to walk across the second sky. He turned and glanced at me. He saw me clinging to the eucalyptus and laughed.

I closed my eyes and flung myself forward. My fingers bit, and I hauled myself onto the carpet. I tried not to look down. I tried to ignore the vibrating branches. I crawled.

He was moving much faster than I was, disappearing into the night. I slung the pack off my back and took out the Wildey.

Starlight reached us here above the canopy, and the darkness was not so utterly complete as it was down below. Even so, the red laser beam was as brilliant as a light show in Central Park. It lit up the small of Nozawa's back, right between the kidneys.

"Behind you," I called.

He turned and saw the brightness in my hands. He looked down.

His expression froze. The starlight glinted in his eyes. Staying low to the carpet, I crept forward.

"It's a laser. It makes it impossible to miss. It's attached to an eleven millimeter handgun. Do you have any idea what a big hole an eleven millimeter slug makes?" My voice was as loud as a cannon.

He stared at me without answering. He was trembling, I could feel it in the branches beneath me.

"It was you at the power station, wasn't it?"

"They were my men. I wasn't there."

"I killed three of them."

"Yes."

"Then you know I won't hesitate to kill you unless you answer my questions. Who killed Joel Tinker?"

"He was a fool. He should have taken the money. He would have been rich."

"Did you kill him?"

"No."

"Who did?"

"He had it coming, whoever it was."

"Are you telling me you don't know? Think about the feeling of lead in your kidneys. Think about looking down at an empty hole where your heart should be."

He turned away for a moment, then faced me again. "I don't know who killed him."

"Did you steal the map from my case?"

"You are as big a fool as he was."

"The fool holding the gun."

"Kimura-*sama* should have killed you in his home."

"He's too smart for that. Now, start walking towards me. We're going down together, nice and easy."

He took a step towards me, then suddenly dropped, flattened himself against the branches, and tried to roll. It was hard to see him. I tried to light up the carpet with the laser, but he disappeared between the layers of wood and leaves. I fired at where I had last seen him. The sound was a thousand times as loud as my voice had been, but not so much louder than his taunting laugh. I crept forward some more. I scanned the carpet floor. I reached for the pocketscope, but realized that I would have to free a hand to use it and that meant standing up.

I rose to my feet shakily, the scope in one hand, the Wildey in the other. I made for the spot where Nozawa had stood only seconds before.

He was gone. I pivoted slowly, searching the scraggly horizon. I looked a little higher, thinking that perhaps he had caught another tree trunk skyward. I had nearly completed my second image-enhanced sweep when I felt a hand on my foot and I went down.

I struggled to get free of his grip, not knowing exactly where he was or how to reach him through the branches. He began a sawing tug, trying to pull me through the top layer of the horizontal growth. I lost my hold on the pocketscope and it dropped. I gripped the Wildey tighter, still trying to fend him off with my feet.

And then there was a sudden glimpse of pale flesh and I knew it was his face. Teetering on a nest of branches thirty feet above the rain forest floor, I mustered my finest heel kick.

"This is for Joel Tinker," I said.

My heel exploded through the tangle of leaves and caught him squarely on the chin. I heard his jawbone crack and saw his glinting eyes roll back.

That instant of unconsciousness cost him his grip on the branches and his grip on life.

My eye couldn't follow him all the way down, but my ears could hear him scream.

# Chapter 31

THERE WAS MORE material missing from Julie's blouse than was required for the sling she had fashioned for her broken arm, but I figured she'd reveal whatever she wanted to in time. She was weaker than she had sounded when she had called to me from the cave, but she could walk. We set out for the river.

"I want to see the body," she said flatly.

"I'm not sure I can find it in the dark."

"I'm not leaving until I see his body."

"He won't be a pretty sight. He fell a long way."

"I want to see him."

"You want to be sure he's dead, don't you?"

"Yes."

"Did he hurt you?"

"Please. Just take me to his body."

I kept a tight grip on Julie's arm, bending low to identify the broken foliage that marked the path I had taken in pursuit of Nozawa. It was a surprisingly short hike to the tree I had scaled to reach the horizontal growth, but I was lost once I was there.

"There's no trail from here on in," I explained.

"Well, which direction did you go?"

I pointed out my best guess, but the forest floor was thick with ferns.

"You sure you want to do this?"

"Ferns are easy," she said, muscling her way through the fronds with her good shoulder.

She was right. The ferns gave way readily, but I found the pocketscope essential, because the growth above us obscured the starlight. It was too dark for zen walking.

I identified the spot where Nozawa had fallen at the same time Julie did, but we used different clues. The nightscope revealed a bright ring to me, caused by the hole in the blanket above. She found the depression in the leaves. Neither of us found the body, but we both found the trail of blood.

"He isn't dead. He's alive and he's going to do it to me again," she whispered in horror.

"He's dead."

"He's not dead. He's alive. He's incredibly strong, you can't imagine how strong he is. He doesn't look like it but he has this grip . . ."

"He's dead. He probably fell three stories. I heard him scream," I answered, giving her a reassuring squeeze and getting down low in the bush with the scope to my eye.

I followed the trail carefully, looking at broken branches and the bloody trail line, which looked dark and fluorescent through the viewer. It went on and on. I stopped and checked my compass. We were heading away from the river. Julie followed me, breathing, occasionally whimpering. My impression had been that she was strong—Amazonian, even—and

I wondered what Nozawa could have done to her to make her so afraid.

"Branches could have broken his fall. People live when they fall out of airplanes without parachutes. It happens sometimes. You know it does, Waku told me you were a pilot," she said dully.

"He's dead," I repeated.

We found him about then, and he was dead. Both his legs were broken and something smooth and shiny was sticking out of a hole in his belly where some tree must have pierced him on the way down. His hands were cramped trying to stuff whatever it was back in. His eyes were staring wide and his face was torn up by the brambles. He didn't look human. I had seen some things as a policeman—murder, suicides, even fires, which I always thought were the worst of all—but I hadn't seen anything quite as bad as Nozawa. Maybe it was because the other stuff I'd seen was in New York, where very little had ever looked beautiful, and this was Tasmania, where even through electron tubes in the night the beauty would stop your heart.

It had certainly stopped Nozawa's. Julie looked at him for a long time, stared straight at him while I fiddled with my equipment and tried to get a fix on *Phantasm* and the river. She even prodded him with her foot.

The man had to have been something really bad to deserve being kicked after he was dead.

By the time we reached the boat, the sun had started to come up, warming the rain forest like a microwave attacking a bag of popcorn. Everything around us seemed to sit up and take notice of the dawn. The dew receded almost visibly from the leaves, particularly in the long white strips where the sun first fell. The thin layer of mist over the surface of the river rose from the heat, and then we were at the tie line and I was shouting for Waku and he was out and she was taking to being wrapped in his arms as if nothing whatsoever was broken—not her will, not her arm, not anything.

Waku cleaned her up in the front cabin, using his Buck knife to cut away pieces of her tattered clothes. Then he took a rag, started gently at her toes, and moved upwards, gently until he had removed every trace of the forest. He gave her fresh clothes—his own fit her remarkably well—dressed her wounded arm as best he could, picked the last bug out of her hair, and shampooed her under the galley faucet while brewing hot coffee and feeding her rolls.

Pullman seemed genuinely impressed, and he made her a proper breakfast after that, or at least what he considered a proper one: toast and eggs and more coffee. While all this went on, I radioed all the news to Isabelle, who arranged for a doctor to meet us at the dock.

Finally Waku allowed me near her, and while Pullman fired up the engines and hauled up the anchor, I got to ask some questions.

"He forced you to fly for him?"

"Yes."

"He was a little man. How did he force you?"

"He had a gun."

"He was after the tiger?"

"He had a map."

"Which he stole from the detective's suitcase," said Waku, taking her hand.

"What happened to your plane?"

"I was flying, he was looking at the map, and then

out the window and then back at the map, telling me where to go. Then I noticed that he was, you know, looking at me. Then he tried to touch me," she shivered.

"You fought?"

"I distracted him, then tried to take away the gun."

"And it went off."

She nodded.

"Into the cowling?"

"Forward, toward the nose. I don't know exactly what it hit but we started going down."

"And you never radioed Melbourne?"

"He wouldn't let me when we took off. After that there was no time."

I sat quiet for a minute, taking it all in.

"Did he say anything about Dr. Tinker?" I asked.

"Nothing. He just wanted the tiger. All he got was me."

She started to cry about then, and Waku took her in his arms again and led her wordlessly to the front bunk where I had been holed up. I couldn't bring myself to ask her if she ever saw anything with stripes.

# Chapter 32

THE LOCAL DOCTOR met us at the landing near Macquarie House and ushered Julie into his car and off to his clinic. Waku went along, and rang us at the inn within minutes to tell us that the elbow was the culprit, but that Julie would be fine in six weeks. While Divac prepared lunch, I got on the phone with Pennington.

"I'll need a statement," he said.

"And a statement you shall have. But I'm not driving back to Hobart to give it to you."

"You killed a man, Mr. Dark. You'll damn well drive where and when I tell you."

"I didn't kill anybody. A guy fell in the forest while climbing a tree. Ms. Iringili is injured, and I'm exhausted. Send a local man over and he can take our depositions."

I hung up the phone and went to soak in a hot bath. When I came downstairs I found a bright and composed Julie Iringili talking a mile a minute to a mousy-looking cop who wrote down every word she said as gospel and never once looked her in the eye. He took my statement as well, uncomfortable at my description of Nozawa's injuries and utterly confused by my directions to the body.

Isabelle sat by Julie at the table, sharing a female connection that excluded even Waku.

"Nozawa told me he didn't kill Tinker," I said.

"Believe him. He bragged about the world to me. If he'd done it, I would know," said Julie.

"So he was out there trying to save his boss five million," said Waku.

"And make brownie points for himself," Isabelle added.

"A true entrepreneur," remarked Pullman, while Divac served up long strips of Tasmanian salmon covered by exotically spiced hollandaise and lying on a bed of spinach. I sat waiting patiently for my vegetables and was pleasantly surprised by a carrot *quiche*.

"Soy milk, no cheese, no butter," Divac said, crossing his arms insecurely, watching my face for a reaction.

I tasted it and smiled. It was worthy of the best vegan emporia in New York or Los Angeles.

"Delicious. Thank you for your trouble; you're a gifted man," I said.

Divac beamed and Pullman smiled and so did I. But it was a hollow smile, because, although I was starting to have a pretty good idea about some things, I still wasn't sure who had killed Joel Tinker.

After lunch I stole a bottle of *cabernet sauvignon* from Pullman's cellar and led Isabelle out to the Fairlane. We took the road north and east out of town until we reached the huge dunes of the ocean beach.

I kept the wine hidden under my pile jacket as I escorted her up and over the hills of shifting sand and out onto one of the most forbidding coastlines in the world.

The wind blew her multihued blonde hair back like a streamer, exposing the perfect line of her jaw and blowing her scarf aside to reveal the translucent skin of her throat and the blue arteries that kept it smooth and nourished. We laced fingers and walked along the beach, the wine bottle heavy in my pocket. A fine salt crust formed on her lips, and I gently wiped it off. She smiled.

"This isn't turning out like you thought it would, is it?"

"I'm glad we found Julie."

"Was it difficult with Nozawa?"

"It wasn't difficult. I followed him, he fell, he died."

"I'm sure there's a little more to it than that."

"Not really. What counts is that he swore he didn't kill Joel Tinker, and I believed him."

"*Did* you kill him?"

"I kicked him, he fell."

"And you still don't know who killed Tinker?"

I shook my head, squinting against the growing wind, watching a thick head of clouds build up over the southern Indian Ocean.

"It's going to storm," I said.

"It always seems to storm here."

"That's why it's so green. That's why the people are the way they are."

"You mean that they don't talk much and they have deep lines on their face?"

I put my arm around her waist and tucked my fingers into her jeans. I led her away from the ocean and into the shelter of a perfect little nook in the dune grass. I took off my coat and produced the wine. She smiled.

"You mind drinking from the bottle? I wanted it to be a surprise."

I turned around to lay my coat down so we'd have somewhere to sit, and when I turned back there were two crystal glasses in her hand and she was already at work on the cork. I must have had some stupid look on my face.

"You forget. I *know* you, buddy boy," she said.

So she popped the cork, and I tasted and poured the wine, and we watched the waves get bigger and the sky get darker, and then we watched each other, and I reached over and brought her closer.

Her kiss tasted like salty *cabernet,* which is actually quite good if the setting is right. I pushed her gently down onto my coat and began to unbutton her blouse.

"It's cold," she whispered.

"Not for long," I whispered back. The wind took my words and her cries and flung them hard and fast out over the fast-moving currents and down towards Antarctica, where I knew no one would ever hear them except maybe the penguins.


When we got back to Macquarie House, Waku told me I had missed a call from Captain Rignola.

"It was worth it," I said.

When I called Rignola, Riley answered the phone. He seemed to be more familiar with my name this time, because he put me right through.

"Where are you getting your information?" my former captain demanded.

"Here and there. Digging around. Detective work, you know."

"I don't know what the hell's happening to you over there. You were never any *good* at detective work."

"I was a hell of a shooter," I reasoned.

"But you were too impatient to be a door knocker."

"A friend of mine is dead. I want to know why."

"You saying it's just luck about the parrots?"

"What about them?"

"Fish and Game says your man Kimura's an assistant curator at the New York Zoological Park. That lets him take out all the Puerto Rican Amazon parrots he wants."

"An appointment arranged by Stanley Winston?"

"Joel Tinker's boss?"

"Call it another lucky guess."

"Goddamn it, Nestor, if you weren't over there I'd have you over here."

"Call me triply lucky," I said and hung up the phone.

I called Chitose at Interpol next. He took the call at once.

"You said Kimura's the head of an industrial group. Any timber holdings?"

"It's a conglomerate. I don't know."

"Will you check while I hold?"

"It may take a few minutes. You want me to call you back?"

"I'd like to know now. I can't afford to hang up."

While he was gone I listened to the hum of fiber optics. It reminded me of the sound of Joel Tinker's last call. That seemed like eons ago.

Chitose came back on the line in five minutes.

"Nothing in the conglomerate," he reported.

"What about his family?"

Chitose sighed.

"I'm going to give you Kimura. Now hold up your end," I said.

"This better be good," he replied and signed off for another five minutes.

It was worth the wait.

"Bingo. Kimura's family owns Nagasaki Milling and Pulping. Now will you tell me what you're onto?"

"Giuseppe Rignola of NYPD tells me that Kimura's an assistant curator at the Bronx Zoo in New York. You might want to talk to him about what it takes to become a legal smuggler. And while you're at it, check out a Lieutenant Pennington in Hobart. He's in Kimura's pocket."

# Chapter 33

TEN MINUTES EARLIER, I had felt that my pieces weren't even on the board. Now I felt like master of the game. Isabelle watched the change in my demeanor with fascination as I put through a call to John Bilkes at Pan Pacific Paper. He asked after Arnet Pichaud, and I confessed I hadn't spoken to him in days.

"You're still in Australia?" he sounded surprised.

"Vacationing in Tasmania."

"Good Lord. It's a bloody wasteland down there. If you had asked me I could have fixed you up with an island in the Whitsundays. That's off the Great Barrier Reef. Lovely time of year for water sports. I know a man in the hotel business."

"Who do you know in the newspaper business?"

"I'm the man to know in the newspaper business, Mr. Dark. Everybody knows *me.*"

"I mean the press."

"Ah. I see."

"Heard of a company called Nagasaki Milling and Pulping?"

"Who hasn't? They get most of our chipped wood."

"Well, it's owned by a guy who lives on a lake near Mt. Bandai."

"Everyone in the business has heard that too. He's a tough bastard. Tell me something I *don't* know."

"All right," I said, still wincing at the fact that I'd been too stupid to see the obvious. "He's planning on taking over Tasmanian logging. Going to pressure the state government to open up the parklands and hit on existing contracts in the southwest."

There was a long pause.

"This information is reliable?"

"So reliable I think it should be reported to someone of influence in the press by someone of influence in the business. I think it's an important public opinion issue for the Australian people. Like I said at our meeting, I think Australian timber should belong to Australia."

"I'm sure I agree. I thank you very much for your call, Mr. Dark, and I hope we have the opportunity to do business soon."

"Oh, Mr. Bilkes?"

"Yes?"

"I was thinking of doing some investing," I mused.

"If you're asking my opinion, I should think that tomorrow might be a good day to make a very short term expression of your confidence in Australian logging technology," he answered immediately.

"Goodbye, Mr. Bilkes," I said.

I flashed the receiver without even hanging up and got Arnet Pichaud's New York office on the line.

"I'm afraid he isn't in, Mr. Dark," his secretary informed me.

"I have a very important message, but you must

give it to him verbally. You may not write it down. Not even on your own scratchpad. Is this a secure phone line?''

''Mr. Pichaud has it swept every week.''

''Very well. Listen closely. This is the message. Tell Mr. Pichaud to invest in Pan Pacific Paper today and sell in three days. Is that clear?''

''Pan Pacific Paper today, sell in three days.''

''And I mean *invest*. Do you understand?''

''Of course, sir.''

''And he'll get this message in time to act on it.''

''Absolutely, sir.''

''And you'll forget totally that this call ever took place?''

''I'm afraid Mr. Pichaud isn't in. Could you give me your name again, sir?''

I smiled and flashed for the international line one last time.

Phil Schillerman, the Dark Foundation's Wall Street broker, answered the phone on the second ring.

''Working late?'' I said.

''Who is this?''

''Nestor Dark.''

''Oh, yes, Mr. Dark. On your portfolio, as a matter of fact.''

''Cut the shit, Phil. Are we set up to get into the Pacific Stock Exchange?''

''We haven't done that before for your account, sir, but we can certainly arrange it. I'll send the requisite paperwork over in the morning.''

''Forget the paperwork. I'll sign it when I come back. I'm in Australia now. I want you to buy two million dollars worth of Pan Pacific Paper immediately. Hold it for three days and then turn it.''

"Pan Pacific Paper. That's an Australian company?"

"Good thinking, Phil."

"And you're in Australia now?"

"Correct."

"This wouldn't be something we shouldn't be doing, would it, Mr. Dark?"

"Think I can find a broker who *does* want the commission, Phil?"

# Chapter 34

WHEN ISABELLE REDFIELD came to work for me, she was living in a walkup on Manhattan's Upper East Side. After two months learning the ropes of the Dark Foundation, she took over the engine room, and after six she took the helm for weeks at a time, leaving me free to navigate the waters of major-league philanthropy. Then she moved to a penthouse at United Nations Plaza. She had a great view of the river there, and she threw out the plastic milk carton she had used as a bedside table and the feather factory that had served as a couch.

She threw out a lot of other things, too. I should know, because I helped her. Clothes and shoes and gloves—important because they kept her hands from chapping, and her hands were her living—all went to the homeless in boxes as she dressed for success in the world of high finance.

But even though it clashed dramatically with the polished, sophisticated, one-step-above-yuppie look of her new pad, she refused to give up her treasure chest.

"It's a physical place for my dreams. Whenever I want something, I put a piece of it there. Your ad in the paper, for example. When I saw it, I clipped it out and put it in the chest," she explained.

"And the act of putting something in the chest makes it come true?"

"I hung a glove there when I wanted to model my hands," she defended.

"And what about me? Did you put a picture of me in there too?"

"None of your business, mister," she snapped.

She had a traveling treasure chest too, a small folding wooden box in which she kept portable wish icons. We went up to our room early that night at Macquarie House and she showed me that it contained a postcard of Tasmania.

"Put there before I asked you to come?" I inquired.

"It would have been a waste of wishes to put it in there afterwards."

"What else is in there?" I asked, trying to get my hands on the little locked box.

"Are you dreaming? Carried away by some small successes detecting timber deals? You think I'm going to let you snoop in here?"

"They weren't small successes."

"All right, they weren't small successes."

"They've probably saved this whole area from logging."

"At least from the Japanese."

"At least from the Japanese," I agreed.

"But it would have been better if you could have found the tiger."

"It would be better if I knew who killed Joel Tinker."

She stared at me a while across the bed.

"You've been saying that since I got here."

"I've been feeling it since I left New York. Rignola's right, something *has* been happening to me. Nothing turns out like it used to, like when I was on the force. There's no sense of rightness or order here."

"Seems you've set some things in motion with Kimura's company. That ought to set things right. Besides, a former cop has to get used to disorder. That's what police work is all about, isn't it?"

"It was for the other guys, but never for me. By the time I was called in to train my rifle on somebody, things had gotten as out of control as they were going to get. If some nutcase was going to take hostages, he'd already done it. If he was going to kill a family and then barricade himself in, he'd already done it. Anything bad that was going to happen—except maybe the nutcase himself catching lead—had already gone down."

"So you were the fixer."

"Other guys did the legwork, I just used my trigger finger. Now I'm doing the legwork, but it's not coming out my way."

"Maybe you're learning something about detective work."

"Maybe I'm learning something about myself."

I sat quietly for a moment with my head in my hands. She watched me.

"You want to see something?" she asked brightly. I looked up from the edge of the bed and she unlocked the traveling chest one more time and pulled out a piece of paper cut with scissors. She handed it to me. It was a blurred black-and-white photograph of a thylacine.

"I cut it out of a book and put it in here," she explained.

I handed it back to her.

"Did you learn about chests from Unity?" I asked, referring to the mystic Park Avenue white witch Andrew Dark had loved for years but never married.

She shook her head. "I kept a treasure chest long before I met Unity. Want to see one more thing?"

"I thought I wasn't allowed to look."

"You're not looking, I'm showing. There's a difference."

She unlocked the box again, restored the thylacine and withdrew another piece of paper.

It was a worn and crumpled color photograph, the dyes faded from more than twenty years of ultraviolet rays. It showed a familiar white Rolls Royce convertible alone in the California desert. A thin boy with wiry hair sat proudly at the wheel, his lips pursed in a "V."

"Where did you get this?"

"I found it in Redding. On your bureau."

"You had no right to take it."

"I'm sorry. I just needed a picture of Joel. For my treasure box. That *is* Joel Tinker, isn't it?"

I nodded, cradling the picture.

"Who took the picture?"

"I did. He was saying 'vroom.' We were out in the desert in Uncle Andrew's Rolls Royce."

"The one he didn't want you to sell."

I nodded.

"I didn't know how to drive, but Joel did. We were

in California on vacation. We were only thirteen. We stole the car and drove it all the way to the desert. Uncle Andrew called the police."

"Big trouble, huh?"

"You have no idea."

I handed the photograph back to her.

"You shouldn't have taken it."

"I said I was sorry."

"Joel's picture in your box won't help anything. Joel's gone. It was an invasion of privacy. It makes me feel like I can't trust you alone with my things."

"We still have a little trust issue between us, don't we?" she asked, referring to some things we'd both done while I was on a recent case.

"I trusted you alone with the handsome Czech chef," I responded.

"And I trusted you alone overnight with Graham Pullman on the river," she laughed, taking the picture and putting it back in the treasure chest.

"That's different. I don't like men," I joked back.

"And I don't like gay chefs."

"Gay chefs?"

"Oh come *on* now, Nestor. Don't tell me you didn't know about Divac and Graham?"

# Chapter 35

I FELT THE same way I had felt earlier that day when John Bilkes told me that everyone knew Kimura owned Nagasaki Milling and Pulping. I guess Isabelle could read it all over my face.

"Really, Nestor, you amaze me. You know the most obscure facts and you see the tiniest things that everyone else misses, but the obvious passes you right by," she said, moving closer to me on the bed and taking my face in her hands.

"Story of my life. My report cards at school used to say that. Everyone did, even Uncle Andrew. He used to knock me on the head with his knuckles and tell me I was off in my own world and ask me what it looked like in there."

Later that night Chitose called to say he had gotten the drop on Kimura.

"The parrots were the key," he said.

"So you've closed him down?"

"Kimura's a rich man. We arrested him, but he won't serve any time. He'll be out within hours."

"Bribes or lawyers?"

"Both," Chitose sighed.

"That's wonderful news."

"Does it help you to know that Nagasaki Milling and Pulping stock dropped twenty percent on the Nikei today?"

"Very much. What's happening with his animals?"

"I don't know yet. At the moment, nothing."

"Can I ask a favor in return for the tip?"

"You can ask."

"Can you arrange to disband the collection and ship the individual animals to zoos that need what he's got for breeding?"

"I doubt it. The Japanese authorities are not exactly enlightened when it comes to conservation."

"I'll pay for it."

"What?"

"If you can arrange it, the Dark Foundation will pick up the shipping costs."

"May I ask why you are willing to do this?"

"I really want the animals returned to the gene pool."

"You mean you want to hit Kimura where it hurts. I'll see what I can do."

I rang Rignola to let him know about Kimura, but he'd already heard.

"Thanks for calling to tell me," I said.

"Operator told me it's the middle of the night there."

"You pick up Winston?"

"Riley got him."

"Good old Riley."

"You think he had something to do with Tinker's death?"

"I don't think Winston sold Joel Tinker out. He never figured Tinker'd find shit. He just let him go because it fit in with what Kimura wanted and it didn't cost him a dime. What's going to happen to him?"

"A fine, probably. Maybe he'll lose his job."

The receiver wasn't even cold in its cradle when someone knocked on the door. I opened it a crack. It was Waku.

"Julie's gone again," he said.

"Oh, come *on*."

"She didn't disappear or anything, she just left."

"Tell him to come in," Isabelle called.

He came in and Isabelle looked him dead in the eye.

"What Julie went through? I've been through that," Isabelle said, sitting up in the bed with the sheet tucked under her armpits.

"What?" I asked.

"It changes things. Sometimes you don't want to be around a man for a while. She'll come back."

"We'll all be going home soon. There isn't any coming back," Waku answered.

Isabelle patted the bed and he sat down on the very edge, on her side, not mine. I stood near the door like an intruder.

"There's nothing you can say or do. She's got to work this through herself."

"I cleaned her up with a washcloth," he half-sobbed.

"No washcloth goes deep enough, but it helps that he's dead," she answered.

"She's my brother's friend."

"He may not hear from her for a while, but when he does, she won't speak badly of you."

"Probably won't speak of me at all," said Waku, his face in his hands.

"Where did she go?"

"Devonport. The first flight out in the morning."

"You want to go after her, go ahead," I said.

Isabelle looked at me. Her eyes glistened in the starlight.

Waku shook his head.

"She doesn't need me now—and you do," he answered.

I sat down on the bed with them.

"It's okay. We'll be leaving soon, you said it yourself. You can meet us back in New York."

"You saw the tiger, didn't you?" Waku raised his head to me.

"Can't prove it, can't be sure."

"She saw it. Clear as day."

"She can't prove it either."

"Still don't know who killed your friend?"

"Maybe that doesn't matter anymore," said Isabelle.

"Maybe it does. It would if it were my friend," said Waku.

"Just go ahead after her," I said.

He sighed low and long and got up from the bed and went to the door.

"Love doesn't always seem to work out the way lovers want it to, either," he said.

"Forget the tragic hero. Go ahead after her. Just be with her, and don't ask her for anything at all."

"And then what? We're still going home to a place ten thousand miles away."

"No law about that," said Isabelle.
That got a little smile out of him.
"Go on," I said.
So he went.

# Chapter 36

Obligation can engender guilt, and guilt can engender loyalty. I think that's the way it was for Andrew Dark in the beginning. There he was, living the lift of the bachelor entrepreneur, all the money in the world, complete freedom, no responsibility—and then, all of a sudden, his brother and sister-in-law get themselves wiped out in a car and he's got to contend with a sixteen-year-old kid.

I know that he adopted me out of loyalty to my father. It had to be that, because he had no chance to develop any loyalty to me. He barely knew me. A neat electric train set or a chemistry kit at Christmas were the markers of our relationship. Not that there was anything wrong with that. He was an adult and I was a child. He was my rich uncle. He was always nice to me. He brought pretty young girls to my parents' house for dinner, and sometimes my parents traded judgmental glances about him being a cradle robber, and he would nudge me under the table with his knee or roll his eyeballs in my direction when he caught them doing it, as if to suggest that I was wiser than they were and knew they were just being silly or jealous or both.

But I got a fair taste of how far loyalty could drive a man when he changed his life to fit me in it. He could have sent me to boarding school, he could have hired round-the-clock nannies—with his money he could have done just about anything he wanted to preserve his routine. Instead he got me my own apartment in New York, made sure my refrigerator was stocked and my education was paid for, and told me to show up three times a week for dinner and tell him about my life.

Adjusting to my loss, I thought a rich and generous absentee parent was every teenager's dream. But I got bored and lonely pretty quickly and, to his credit, Andrew Dark sensed it before I turned to gangs or drugs. He let me know in plain English that he cared about me but had no experience as a dad. He was so honest about it, so completely without complexes or anything to hide, that I responded by telling him when I thought he screwed up. He listened, and I did too. I learned when to come over and talk, learned that it was okay to have needs, to tell him I wanted to go to Redding for the weekend, to tell him I was tired of eating alone.

And I got to watch his loyalty to my father transfer to loyalty to me. Some kids at my high school saw his limo pick me up a few times and got the idea that I had pocket money to spread around for their appetites and habits. They weren't poor kids, and when they hit on me, I told them where to go and they let me have it. I didn't show up at Uncle Andrew's for dinner a couple of nights running and he came over to find out why.

Some parents—my own, even—might have gone to the school principal or called the cops, the sort of thing parents do when they're thinking more about their own indignation than what's best for their child. Andrew Dark's solution was different. He scribbled an address on a piece of paper and told me to meet him there the next day after school. I went and it turned out to be a Korean karate *dojang*. He took me inside, introduced me to the *sensei*—a twenty-three-year-old hotshot with the wrong kind of attitude and an awesome set of kicks up his trousers—and left.

I found out quickly enough that Korean Tang Soo Do wasn't the style for me, but not before I learned enough to get my schoolmates off my back. And not before I acquired a taste for the arts which led me to various Chinatown emporia, and finally to Amos Larsen.

That first taste of loyalty, given me when I was young and impressionable, stuck in my soul. Long before Joel Tinker called from Tasmania I was living a loyal life, disbursing what Andrew Dark had accumulated in fifty-eight years and adhering to the principles he had told me were important. Despite the moral benefits that attended the decision, there were times I resented it. At other times I was glad to be able to make a contribution to people's lives, more of a contribution than a sniper's bullet could ever make.

So after Waku left to pursue his girl, I lay in the dim blue light and thought about Joel Tinker and loyalty. Isabelle watched me closely, but I didn't want to talk, so I kept my eyes closed and pretended I was sleeping until finally I was.

Later I awakened, convinced that Uncle Andrew's ghost had returned. I checked every inch of the room, as thoroughly as an exterminator might, but I was alone except for Isabelle, who appeared as nothing more than an uneven lump under the covers. The clock by the bed said 5:00 A.M.

A faint clicking noise drew me to the window and I noticed lights on in the garage halfway down the driveway. I pulled on pants and a shirt, hooked my fingers around a pair of shoes, and crept quietly out of the room.

It was much colder outside than I had expected. The sharp gravel stabbed my feet, but instead of putting on the shoes I drove my soles hard against the stones, letting them set off the acupressure points in my feet like little firecrackers. The pain, the cold, and the nervous stimulation awakened me completely, and by the time I reached the glowing side window of the garage I was as alert as a skydiver on his first jump.

Graham Pullman was in there, sitting on a bench pulled up to a worktable, the waterlogged map I'd taken from Julie Iringili's plane spread out in front of him. The storage cabinet next to him was wide open. A six-foot topographical map of the Lower Gordon was taped to the inside of the door, the land tan on a white background, the rivers printed in red.

The cabinet was chock full of surveillance equipment. Through the cracked and dusty window I could see half a dozen 35mm cameras with long lenses, several pairs of binoculars, a spotting scope, and the large dishes of what I assumed were parabolic microphones. Every few seconds, Pullman would reach idly over and depress the electronic shutter of a professional-looking Nikon on his table, causing the motor drive to fire and make the clicking sound that had carried through the ultra-still Tasmanian night and wakened me from a dreamless sleep.

I don't know how long I stood watching Pullman tracing lines with his finger, cleaning out the inside of his lower lip with his thumb, and firing off that electronic Nikon. All I know is that I was still trying to make sense of what I was seeing when I felt cold metal touch my temple and I dropped my shoes on the driveway.

# Chapter 37

DIVAC SHOVED ME hard against the side of the garage, scraping my face on the weathered shingles. His chef's apron did a pretty good job of disguising what was obviously a very powerful body.

"Why are you spying?" he demanded.

"I heard a noise. I was curious. I came downstairs. Now take that shotgun away from my temple."

Pullman's head jerked up at the exchange, and he scrambled to fold the map and kick the camera cabinet shut.

"Who's there?" he shouted, looking wildly about.

Divac attempted to drag me to the side door, but I relaxed completely in his grasp, making myself dead weight.

"Walk," he cursed.

"Take the gun away from my head," I replied calmly, folding my hands across my chest.

By way of answer he jammed the barrel even more violently against my flesh. My tongue dried to gauze in an instant and my mouth felt like cotton. Pullman opened the door just before we reached it, his lanky frame casting a long black shadow with a yellow halo on the rough gravel.

"What's going on here? Divac! What are you doing?"

Divac pushed me again, and I stumbled past Pullman and into the workshop.

It was far larger than it had appeared from the window, and even more completely stocked. One whole wall was covered by what appeared to be miniature rockets.

"I caught him spying at the window," Divac said gruffly, still brandishing the shotgun.

"This is not a way to treat a guest," said Pullman.

"Tell him to put down the gun," I said.

"I caught him spying at the window, I tell you," Divac repeated.

"You've been hunting the tiger all along," I said.

"So you've found me out, Mr. Dark." Pullman gave a faint, sick smile.

"I'm not sure what I've found."

He nodded, gestured at the rockets.

"They carry cameras aloft. Not as sophisticated as your submarine, I'm afraid, but they give a much wider view."

"They can't see through thick forest."

"I don't believe the tigers live in thick forest."

"And those? Parabolic microphones?"

"Yes indeed, but I can show you better than that."

He reached for a small metal box on the shelf next to the umbrella-shaped parabolic mike. A clear plastic rod protruded from it, as did a pair of headphones.

"A laser listener. We used them in SWAT. I thought they only worked against a pane of glass," I said.

"The forest canopy moves like glass," Pullman answered, clearly disappointed that I was familiar with the technology.

"Why are you telling him these things?" Divac wailed.

"You haven't found a tiger yet, have you?" I asked.

"Found one? Yes I believe I have."

"Proof?" I gestured at the camera equipment.

"Regrettably, no."

"Did you kill Joel Tinker?"

"Why are you talking to him? He is the enemy!" Divac screamed.

"I'm nobody's enemy. Tell him to put down the gun," I said.

"Put the gun down, Divac," Pullman said gently.

The chef paid no attention.

"The inn must have cost you a fortune," I said.

"Don't talk about the money. He's the one who's going to take it away!" Divac raved.

"It didn't start out that way. I was going to do most of the work myself," Pullman confessed, staring at the shotgun.

"You didn't anticipate the recession."

"It's not a recession in Australia, Mr. Dark, it's a depression. We calculated break-even at four years of fifty percent occupancy. You are only our second guest this week."

"I'm not competing for the tiger money. In fact, I've offered an additional million. I thought you knew that. Now tell him to put the gun down," I commanded.

For a moment, looking at Divac, I could almost

see what Pullman saw in him. Standing under the overhead door he looked tortured, beautiful, angelic, and absolutely insane.

The gun stayed aimed at my face.

# Chapter 38

IF PULLMAN HAD not moved to close the door against the gathering Tasmanian dawn, Waku might not have been able to raise the P-88 Walther in time to stop Divac from shooting me. As it happened, Waku was quick, Divac was distracted, and both Pullman and I were shocked.

"Drop the shotgun," Waku boomed, his voice as large and clear as mine had been when I faced Nozawa across the horizontal growth. There was something about the air in Tasmania that made the light shine and sound waves skip like happy children.

Divac froze.

"Looks like a stalemate," Pullman observed, shifting uncomfortably against what I knew must have been one cold German barrel.

"This is a P-88 Walther. It's the finest automatic handgun in the world. Without reloading, it shoots more nine millimeter lead than it takes to fill a man's head," said Waku.

"Forget the fancy pistol. This is a shotgun," said Divac.

"I thought you went after Julie," I said.

"I got halfway to Devonport when I realized I was thinking more about me than about her. She needs the space. She knows where to find me," Waku replied.

"A fortunate conclusion, as it turns out," I said.

"Would everybody please put their guns down now?" Pullman implored.

"Nobody else is going to take our money!" Divac screamed. He moved unsteadily closer to me, the shotgun bouncing in his hands.

"What are you saying?" Pullman paled.

"I stopped the other one and I'm going to stop this one. We've worked too hard to let them stop us now!" Divac cried.

I guess we all realized what he meant about the same time, because the room got as quiet and still as a photograph.

"Who did you stop?" Pullman asked.

"That Tinker. You know he found the tiger."

"You *stopped* Joel Tinker?" I asked, turning slowly so that I could watch Pullman's reaction and Divac's gun at the same time.

"Macquarie House is Graham's life," Divac said, his voice breaking.

"Graham's still got his life," said Waku, shifting his gun slightly.

Pullman closed his eyes.

"You think you can just come here with your money and your machines and take away *our* future?" Divac's Czech accent was becoming more and more apparent under the strain.

"You shot Joel Tinker, and he died all alone in a phone booth," I said.

"He had it coming. I would have killed the Japanese, too. They tried to find the tiger too, so they wouldn't have to pay. Nobody would leave us alone," Divac screamed.

Pullman let out a long, low moan.

"The Japanese never wanted there to *be* a tiger," I said sadly. "They were trying for a timber contract. They figured if nobody could find one with a five million dollar reward, the species was really extinct and the Greens wouldn't be able to use the tiger as an excuse not to clear the land."

*"Nobody* wanted to find that tiger," said Waku.

"You *killed* Dr. Tinker?" Pullman whispered.

"He was after our money," Divac replied.

Pullman slumped in pain despite Waku's Walther. Divac's eyes had been trained on my torso, where his gun was pointing, but they flickered away when Pullman collapsed.

I took that moment to leap sideways so that the barrel pointed at air. I ducked low and used a sweep technique from White Crane kung fu to take Divac down. The shotgun went off, blowing a hole in the roof of the garage and letting in the light.

I wrestled the gun away, broke the barrel and put the shell on Pullman's workbench next to the map.

Waku shoved the Walther in his pocket.

When Isabelle appeared a few moments later, her hair awry, her eyes wild, Pullman and Divac were on the ground by the cameras and Pullman was rocking the chef back and forth in his arms.

"I just wanted everyone to leave us alone," Divac sobbed.

Pullman's bony hands covered the side of Divac's face with his caresses.

"Shh. It's over now. Everything is all right."

But it wasn't.

# Chapter 39

THREE MONTHS LATER, the first microfiber blanket hit my desk as silently as a feather. I looked up from the *Wall Street Journal* to see Isabelle standing there with a big smile on her face.

"Go ahead and pick it up," she urged.

I took it in my hands. It felt strangely alien and supple.

"Crumple it up! Wring it like a sponge," she exhorted.

I did. When I let go, it resumed its shape with no trace of a wrinkle.

"Now put it on."

I wrapped it around me. Before I could stop her, Isabelle poured half a cup of hot coffee over my shoulders. I heard it splat against the back of my desk chair. I shot forward before it stained my suit.

"Thanks a lot."

"Check out the blanket."

I placed it on my blotter. The few drops of coffee that hadn't run off adhered to the fabric as tentatively is ladybugs. Nothing seeped through or caused a stain. Isabelle reached over and patted it with a napkin. When she finished, the blanket was as good as new.

"It doesn't even hold the heat," she beamed.

I felt it and she was right.

"Go ahead with the underwear," I said.

"Sheila Greenstock's outside. About the health food for children?"

"Bring her in."

I opened a couple of letters while Isabelle went to get her friend. One was a quarterly report from Phil Schillerman, the broker who had handled the Australian timber transaction. It showed a profit of $360,000 for the three-day stock turnaround. Another was a letter from the principal of the high school where Andrew Dark had sent me. They were starting a science scholarship in memory of Joel Tinker, the better to help an underprivileged youth enjoy a first class high school education and two summer internships in pure research fields. There was a business reply card attached, with little boxes marked $25, $50, $100 and "other." I put a tick by "other" and wrote out a three, a six, and four zeroes. Then I sat waiting for Sheila and thinking about Joel.

Sheila Greenstock was a cherubic woman with sparkling blue eyes, wide hips, and a butch haircut. She pumped my hand vigorously.

"I brought some Yankee bean soup for you to taste," she said.

"They used to serve Yankee bean soup at my high school," I muttered.

"The Yankee bean soup they served you was probably made from canned beans, full of preservatives and sweetened with molasses, which is nothing more than sugar, which we now know contributes to learning disabilities. Here, taste this.''

She pulled a little crockpot out of her cavernous handbag, unclipped the metal retaining ring, and spooned a generous slurp across the desk and right into my mouth.

I told her it was delicious and I meant it.

"Isabelle says you need fifteen thousand to get off the ground," I said.

She pulled a sheaf of papers from the same purse and laid them carefully on the desk.

"I'm proposing a series of manufacturing and marketing tests. The investment is pay-as-you-go. If at any time it looks like the venture won't be profitable, you can withdraw and only be out the test money."

I held her eye a moment and then looked down at the business plan. It was well thought out and clearly presented, relying less on a persuasive introduction than many such plans and more on a convincing column of numbers.

"Sheila used to be an accountant," Isabelle reminded me anxiously.

I spent a few more minutes with the plan.

"You have the money, Sheila. But there's one condition," I said at last.

"Which is?"

"Find another name for that soup."

When Sheila was gone, I sat back in my chair and thought some more about Joel and stared at the cabinet where I used to keep some air pistols and a few of Andrew Dark's more valuable toys before I built the toy room. I got up and walked over to it, took out

he small duffel I had thrown in there upon my return
rom Tasmania. I unzippered it and dumped the con-
ents on my desk.

Some of Joel's clothes were there. I laid my hand
on them for a moment and then gently dropped them
n the wastebasket. His beat-up stainless steel Rolex
was there too. I set it, gave it a shake to get it going,
and strapped it on my wrist.

There was a videotape there as well, the one the
ittle submarine had shot. I walked over to the VCR,
oopped it in, turned on the TV and returned to my
lesk. I put my feet up and relaxed to the sight of yard
after yard of soothing Tasmanian riverscape. My eyes
grew heavy, but still I watched, thinking of Divac and
Pullman and Waku and Julie, but most of all thinking
about Joel Tinker, on the other side of the world, all
alone in that telephone booth.

I don't know whether I dozed, or how long the tape
kept running. All I know is that right near the end of
he run, right before the tape ran out somewhere along
he lower Gordon River, a pair of incandescent eyes
stared out of a head that looked like a hyena atop a
oody that looked for all the world like a certain Asian
cat. The thylacine's front feet were in the river, where
 guess he'd been drinking, but the little periscope
lidn't seem to scare him. He just gave it a measured
ook, took one more lap with his giant tongue, and
oped easily off, disappearing into the forest as grace-
ully as a ghost.

I made a tiny temple out of my hands and prayed.

# GRITTY, SUSPENSEFUL NOVELS
# BY MASTER STORYTELLERS
# FROM AVON BOOKS